BARE
NERVE

BARE NERVE

KATHERINE GARBERA

BRAVA

KENSINGTON PUBLISHING CORP.
http://www.kensingtonbooks.com

This book is dedicated to my sisters,
Donna Sutermeister and Linda Beardsley-Harris,
who when we were growing up always made me feel
like we were the superheroes, superspies,
and really whatever else we put our minds to.
This book is just like the adventures
we used to dream of while
we played in our backyard.

Acknowledgments

I'd like to thank Mary Louise Wells, who is not only a good friend but is also a great critique partner.

I also have to give a shout-out to my Romex friends who are always supportive at every stage of the writing process and who always give me a safe place to call home.

Lastly to my family, Rob, Courtney, and Lucas, who are always happy to discuss plots at the dinner table and make emergency runs to the bookstore to buy more research books.

Chapter One

"Wake me up inside" blared from the speakers of her MacBook Pro as Anna Sterling traced back to the source the money that had been embezzled from AlberTron. The embezzler was a sophisticated criminal and a bit wilier than others she'd encountered while working for Liberty Investigations.

But she was the best at what she did, and there wasn't a computer system created that she couldn't find her way into.

She liked computers so much better than people. It was easier to deal with a logical computer program than to try to figure out people and their random decisions.

The client Liberty Investigations was working for was AlberTron, which designed and manufactured computer-processing chips and was the foremost leader in that technology. They were in high demand and making an insane amount of money each year.

Which was why Anna was sure the embezzler figured the company wouldn't miss a few million out of the till.

"Did you find anything yet?"

Anna glanced up at the doorway. Even though she loved computers and working with them, she really was trained to be an operative. That's what her partner Charity Keone expected. Charity hovered in the doorway, an expectant look on her face.

"Not yet," Anna said. "But I feel like it's going to break soon."

"Thank God. I told Daniel last night if I had to spend one more day in the office I'd go nuts."

"I think we all got that impression when you beat the stuffing out of that punching bag this morning."

"Well . . . Daniel's not scheduled to be back in DC for another two weeks, and I'm not used to all this inactivity."

"You used to be," Anna said before she could stop herself. Damn, had she sounded bitter or resentful?

Charity grinned, her eyes sparkling with secrets she shared only with Daniel. "That's right. But I've changed. I can't explain it too fully, because I'm still me, but it's like a part of myself I didn't know about is suddenly alive."

Anna was happy for her friend. Charity had lived alone a long time . . . since the death of her parents when she was in her late teens. "I've heard love can do that."

"Have you ever been in love?" Charity asked.

Anna glanced at her computer screen, but it was still searching and tracking the routes the embezzler had used to cover his tracks. She really didn't want to have a conversation about love.

"Is that too personal?" Charity asked.

Anna shrugged. "I guess not. I'm not sure how to answer it without sounding really cynical."

Charity laughed, and Anna had to smile. "I get where you're coming from . . . so it's a no?"

"Big-time. I'm not sure I can trust any man enough to love him."

"I know what you mean. Daniel is honestly the last man I thought I'd ever fall for."

"He is perfect for you," Anna admitted. He was perfect for Charity because he was strong in the areas Charity wasn't. And because he was devoted to her. Charity had been a top-shelf model as a teenager. She was tall, stacked, and incredibly beautiful, from the tip of her blond head to the bottom of her polished designer heels.

"Yes, he is. Should I leave you to this?"

"Yes, you better. The sooner we know who's behind the missing millions, the sooner we can go to Seattle and apprehend him."

Charity nodded and left the office. Anna sat back in her chair. She smiled to herself at the advanced program she'd written to track the various routes the money took back to the man who'd taken it . . . Ivan Kirch.

"Got him!" she yelled, jumping out of her chair and running into the desk.

"So, who is he?" Justine O'Neill asked as she came out of her office. Justine was tiny, maybe five feet tall, and wore her jet-black hair cut shorter in the back than in the front. She looked like a pixie but fought like a warrior. She had a criminal past and was one of Anna's best friends.

"Ivan Kirch."

"No way. The CFO?"

"Yes. I knew there was something about him that wasn't right," Charity said as she joined them.

A former martial-arts expert, Charity was the least lethal looking of the three of them. Because Charity looked like arm candy, she pulled bodyguard duty for heads of state and other dignitaries more often than Anna or Justine.

"I agree. I didn't really like the way he acted when we talked to his staff. He should have been more cooperative," Anna said.

"I thought he was just being a prick because he's a guy," Justine said.

"What's a prick?" Piper asked.

All three women glanced over at the doorway. They weren't used to having a child in their midst. The ten-year-old girl was the daughter of Justine's fiancé, Nigel Carter. And very precocious.

"A not-nice man," Anna said as she watched Justine flounder for a definition that would suit a ten-year-old.

Justine mouthed the word *thanks*. It was funny to Anna to see her normally so self-assured friend struggle with the young girl.

"What do you all do, now that you've found him?" Piper asked.

"We'll each have something to do. We need to talk to Sam and get everything in place. Can you entertain yourself for a little while, Pip?"

"Sure! I'll be fine on my own until Daddy comes to pick me up."

Justine nodded, and the girl went back to Justine's office.

Anna couldn't help staring at Justine, wondering at the changes in her friend. Charity was engaged now, too. And Anna couldn't help feeling like things were changing in their little group. Once the others got married, what would she do?

Sam wouldn't keep a one-person team, and marriage changed operatives. She'd seen it happen before with her own brother. Once he was an MI-5 field operative, but now he worked behind a desk directing a highly effective team. Anna didn't understand how being in the office suited her brother, but he'd said having a wife and child made him vulnerable in the field—he had too much to lose.

Now Charity and Justine were the same way.

"Anna?"

"Yes?"

"I asked if you wanted me to get Sam on the line and let him call Marcus Ware of AlberTron?"

"Yes, that would be good. I've already got a prelim file on Kirch from when we took the job. But I want to make sure I haven't missed anything."

"What's there to miss?" Justine said. "He's a dirty bastard who's stealing from the company, and now his number is up."

"What I think Justine is saying is that he's an executive for a computer company—how much more could there be to find?" Charity asked.

Anna didn't know, but she didn't like leaving any stone unturned. "Daniel and Nigel were both executives as well."

"True enough," Justine said. "When are we having a conference with Sam?"

"I'll go call him now. I'm thinking thirty minutes. Is that long enough for you to get your background info together, Anna?"

"It is. I've got most of the information auto-feeding into a report right now. I'll e-mail you both the file when it's complete."

Anna went back into her office. It was a nice one, with windows along one wall that overlooked the Mall area of Washington, DC. She'd always liked this city, and though as a British citizen she didn't feel a sense of American patriotism, she had always admired Americans and their pride and attitude.

"Got a sec?" Charity asked from the doorway.

Anna glanced down at the screen she was working on. She'd just logged in to the Interpol Web site, using their databases to search for information on Ivan Kirch. She had about two minutes while the database pulled information on her search from all its associated networks. "I've got about two minutes."

"That's all I need."

Charity closed the door behind her and sat down in one

of the guest chairs, though no one ever visited their office, so guest chairs were kind of superfluous.

"Are you okay?" Charity asked after a minute. Charity's expressive face fell into lines of concern, but not the kind Anna had ever seen when she was worried about a knotty case.

"Of course. Why do you ask?"

"You seem different lately."

Anna shook her head, feeling the weight of her hair against her back. She needed a haircut, she thought. But she liked the length and the fact that she could put it in a braid and not worry about it when they were on an op.

She really didn't want to talk personal stuff, but if Charity had noticed a difference, it was a good bet Justine had, too. Better to settle things now than upset the balance of the team at a crucial point in an op.

"I'm not the one who has changed," she said quietly.

Charity nodded. "Is that the problem?"

Anna shook her head. "No, not a problem. Listen, Charity, if we're going to meet with Sam soon, I need to be gathering information." What could she say? She couldn't mention the fact that with Justine and Charity settling down, she felt like the Lone Ranger. She'd sound like a whiner, and that was something she flat-out refused to do.

"Bullshit," Charity said.

"Excuse me?"

"If I know you, and I do, you're already done gathering information. You never need any extra time to complete anything."

"In this case you're wrong. I want to find out more about Ivan's past. Did you know the man doesn't show up in any databases until nineteen ninety-six?"

"So?"

"Where was he before that? I think he must have an alias. I'm trying to track that down."

"How can you do it?"

"Through pictures. A fingerprint would be ideal, but I don't have one. AlberTron isn't implementing their new biotech security system until next quarter."

Charity smiled. "I'm glad to see you're still the same here . . . on the job."

"Of course I am. Charity, my issues are my issues. They have nothing to do with you or Justine. And I won't let them get in the way of the job." Even though Justine was still in her own office presumably with Piper, Anna needed Charity to pass on to Justine that she was just fine.

"Fair enough. I'll see you in the conference room in a few minutes?"

"Yes."

She needed a few minutes to gather herself before the meeting. She had the feeling Sam was going to say this was the last case. Justine and Charity hadn't said anything, but Anna's gut told her the other women weren't going to want to keep taking dangerous cases—not that embezzling was dangerous.

"I'm here if you want to talk about whatever is troubling you."

"Thanks, Charity. I'll keep that in mind."

As the other woman left, Anna clicked on her iTunes program and found the loudest music she could. She needed something to drown out the thoughts in her head. She settled on AC/DC's "Back in Black." One click, and it blared from the speakers on her laptop.

She stared at the computer. Life was so much easier when you didn't have to deal with people. Gathering information, finding bad guys, apprehending them through the ether of the Internet was what she liked.

Computers didn't dredge you through the messy emotions that came from working with people. If she'd just sent an e-mail to Justine and Charity about capturing the embezzler, she wouldn't have had to endure that conversation with Charity.

And honestly, how was she supposed to tell one of her best friends that her problem was jealousy? Finding Liberty Investigations had been a godsend. Like Charity and Justine, she'd felt for the first time since her childhood that she'd found her place. The one place where she fit in and wasn't an anomaly.

But now that had changed, and once again she was the odd man out.

She needed to tune that out. No matter what happened to the team, she'd always be able to find work. She'd even had an offer from a mercenary they'd used on their last mission in Peru. The only problem with working for a man who took money to fight was her own sense of right and wrong.

Anna wasn't one of those people who saw the gray areas of life. There was right—where people lived within the laws of society—and there was wrong—where people lived like Ivan Kirch, who thought he could get away with stealing 5.3 million dollars.

Anna felt a sense of satisfaction at having caught Kirch and looked forward to the moment when the police arrested him and took him to jail.

She shook her head. Her life had become this job, and these little moral victories were now the biggest thrills she experienced in her life.

She wished sometimes that she were more daring in person. And she knew her life was more exciting than most people's. She was an excellent marksman, a martial-arts expert, and she traveled the world for her job. She went to truly exotic places, too, not just to conference rooms in corporate buildings.

But there were times when her life felt so . . . hollow.

"Anna?"

"Yes?"

"We're ready for you in the conference room."

"I'll be right there," she said.

This place was like home to Anna, and as much as she didn't like the changes that had been taking place lately, she knew that she didn't want to go anywhere else.

Ivan Kirch was a man who had everything, and he knew it. He looked at the picture on his desk of his beautiful red-headed wife and their two sons. The boys had inherited his blond hair and his wife's good looks. They would never have to go to bed hungry or fear their father's hands the way he had.

He had been a rough-looking man until the plastic surgery almost ten years ago. When his boss, Maksim, had been captured by authorities, Ivan had seen his opportunity to take over the business. He promised himself he'd make none of Maksim's mistakes.

The first thing he did was change everything about himself so there would be no connection between his new identity and Demetri Andreev. He'd kept his contacts in the arms-dealing world and continued to act as the middleman in deals. But he'd started small, as he'd known he'd have to.

And he'd needed money.

His journey to America had made sense. It was where Maksim was being held. At first he'd hoped to bribe a jailer to free his friend, but that hadn't been easy. And breaking Maksim out of prison wasn't an option. So he'd walked away from his boss and brother and never looked back.

Sometimes, though, late at night, he did read the articles on the Internet about Maksim . . . the so-called Merchant of Death.

Ivan knew he himself hadn't led a life that was blameless, but today, sitting, in his Seattle office and looking out his window on Puget Sound, he felt a sense of well-being at how far he'd come. And at the fact that his life was exactly as he'd made it.

It was hard to let go of the boy he'd been, and he had clawed his way out of the poverty and violence that had been the Moscow of his youth. He'd been born and raised during the Cold War and had been trained to fight for the Soviet regime against the allied countries. He would have been a good spy if he'd been better at taking orders.

He wasn't a big man. Fighting wasn't something he was good at unless he could level the playing field with a knife or handgun. He liked that about weapons.

Ivan had made it his life's work to make sure wars were fought with weapons—that the poor and downtrodden of the world had the guns and ammo they needed to fight back against their oppressors.

He laughed to himself. He sounded like a saint, which he wasn't. He did it for the money these days. Frieda required a lot of cash to make sure the boys lived their lifestyle. And Ivan didn't mind. Making money was something he was good at.

He had become something of an actor over the years. He was forty-five and had lived longer than he'd ever expected. Most days he was amazed at the life he lived now. Amazed at the softness of this world in Seattle. Most of the computer people were workaholics who thought the business world was cutthroat, but Ivan knew what real cutthroat was. It was knowing that if you screwed up a deal, you were dead. Really dead—not just fired with no hopes of a recommendation.

His intercom buzzed, and he answered it. "This is Ivan."

"Marcus wants to see you in his office."

Ivan glanced at his printed calendar. He wasn't much of a

computer man. As much as he liked being able to check information on the Internet, he didn't use his computer for much more than that. Paper could be burned, but computer hard drives were always traceable.

"We have a one-on-one scheduled for this afternoon, can't he wait for that?"

"I will ask him. Also, your wife called to say that Nica has soccer practice this afternoon at four."

"Make sure that's on my calendar."

"I have."

Less than five minutes later, Tiffany buzzed back. "He'd like to meet with you now."

"Let his office know I'll be there as soon as I can," Ivan said.

"I told him you had a meeting with your staff in fifteen minutes, and he asked that we push it back."

"Very well. Thank you, Tiffany."

"You're welcome, Ivan. I also rescheduled the rest of your day. I'll reprint your calendar and leave it on your desk."

"Thank you."

Ivan hung up the phone and sat back in his chair. He wasn't worried about a meeting with the CEO of the company. Though he had been embezzling money for the last five years, he'd been careful to cover his tracks. And even *he* had an exit strategy.

He did a quick check of his accounts online and saw no red flags, such as holds or pending amounts. He used the money from AlberTron to do initial buys for rebels. Some of the groups he sold weapons to couldn't afford to pay up front, so he covered them at a nice interest rate.

He closed his browser and walked down the hall to his boss's office. He wished sometimes that Maksim could see this. Could see the way Ivan had taken the legacy of all that Maksim had left behind and carved this life out of it.

His brother had been the only one Demetri had ever really cared about. He had his boys now, though, and he hoped they grew up to be as close as he and his brother had been.

But Demetri knew no matter how close the bonds of family, at the end of the day the only one you could count on was yourself.

He'd made his life by taking care of himself, and that was why he was sitting in this plush office and Maksim was rotting in jail.

And as much as he loved his brother and had always looked up to him, Demetri knew there was no way he was going to end up the way Maksim had.

Chapter Two

Anna walked into the conference room and found Charity and Justine already seated in their chairs. Because Sam only communicated with them through the Internet and a one-way video feed, they sat in large, executive-style leather chairs with small laptop desks in front of them.

The far end of the room was equipped with a large flat-screen TV they used to monitor several news feeds. Each of them could upload information from their own laptops to the TV, and Sam often sent them information on the screen when they were all in a meeting like this one.

"Now that you are all here, let's begin," Sam said.

Anna related everything she could find on Ivan Kirch. "I've asked for a search on everyone who's disappeared within a five-year age range of Ivan. I want to see if he has any other connections. On the surface he looks like a family guy who likes a wealthy lifestyle. But to be honest, he isn't spending beyond his salary. I would feel a hell of a lot better about this arrest if we knew what he was using the money he's taken for."

"It may be hookers or gambling," Justine said. "In the initial report we got on him it showed frequent trips to Las Vegas and European gambling hot spots."

"I checked that," Anna said a bit snappishly. "His gambling checks out. He's done a really good job of making it seem as if he's nothing more than an executive."

"I think surveillance would be the best idea. Do we have anyone in Seattle who can do it for us?" Charity asked.

"I'll take care of that," Sam said. "We'll see what we find. I've already contacted Marcus and told him only that we found the leak and asked him to schedule a meeting first thing tomorrow morning so we can talk to him and his executive staff."

"Good. I should find out more about Ivan while we're on the plane," Anna said.

"Law enforcement will meet you all at the airport tonight so you can get the arrest warrants. They will facilitate the arrest," Sam said.

"What time are we leaving?"

"The corporate jet is fueled and ready to go. It's up to you ladies. Just keep me posted."

"We will," Charity said. "Anna, when do you think you'll have what you need?"

"We can leave in an hour or so. I want to make a few calls, but I can get information in the air just as easily as I can here."

"Sounds good," Sam said. "Justine, are you okay to leave that soon?"

"Yes, Nigel is picking up Piper in twenty minutes, so I'm good to go. And no offense, but I'm ready for some action after sitting in the office for the last week."

Sam laughed, and Anna smiled. Justine wasn't really cut out for desk work. Maybe their team wouldn't be breaking up any time soon. Anna would have to see what the next case was and how it affected everyone.

"Anna, I need a word with you," Sam said.

Charity and Justine got up to leave, and Anna relaxed back against her chair. Though they couldn't see Sam, he could see them, and she wanted to at least give the appearance of everything being normal.

"What did you need?" Anna asked.

"I'm here if you need to talk about anything," Sam said.

"Case related? I think this is pretty straightforward."

"No, not case related . . . life related. I know there have been a lot of changes with Charity and Justine lately, and I wanted to be sure you knew that whatever they decide, I'm not closing this office."

"That is good to know, Sam. I'm not ready to retire yet."

"I suspected as much. Are you still happy working here?"

"Yes, of course. Why?"

"I have another team I can move you to if this isn't working for you."

Anna knew Sam had teams working all over the world. She'd done extensive research trying to find his identity when he'd first offered her this job, but all trails led nowhere. Sam Liberty was a man who didn't want to be found.

There were things in her past even Sam didn't know. Things she'd managed to hide from the world but never from herself. And she freely acknowledged that as long as someone wasn't breaking the law, they were entitled to their secrets.

"Thank you for the offer. I was feeling a bit lost with all the changes that have been going on."

"I can understand that."

"It's not a job thing," Anna said. "I really enjoyed this case for AlberTron."

"Marcus has a lot of questions for us. He was convinced it was a competitor and not an inside man. He'd be ecstatic if you could tie Kirch to a competitor."

"I'll try, but so far I can't find any answers I really need. Kirch shows no signs of spending any of the money. I'm still digging."

"That *is* a bit odd, isn't it? We usually see a pattern of spending. Why do you thing we haven't?"

"I think he's hiding another identity, and I have to connect the two. I'm pretty close to unraveling it. I can feel the answer waiting right around the corner."

"You have good instincts for that kind of thing."

Sam rarely complimented any of them. "Thank you."

"You already knew that," Sam said with a wry tone that made her smile.

"Very true. I am the best at this." There was no use being shy about her skills. She was one of the top computer experts in this field, and she knew it.

"I know, Anna."

Her computer beeped as it finished a search, and she glanced down at the screen. She was shocked at what she saw there. Oh. My. God. This wasn't what she'd expected to find. "Sam, we have a problem."

"What is it?"

"Ivan Kirch is also known as Demetri Andreev—the younger brother of Maksim Andreev. Demetri is now the top dog in gun running and black-market weapons sales."

Sam said nothing, but Anna knew it was because he was reading the files she was sending him. She couldn't believe the connection at first. But the information was accurate, and the photos were detailed.

"Several governments have been looking for Demetri. . . ." Sam said. "I need to make a few calls, Anna. Alert the rest of the team to this new development and gather them here in the conference room. We need to hold off on arresting him."

"Why? We know where he is. This is a prime opportunity."

"We don't have clearance to go after him for anything other than embezzling."

"I know that, but why should that matter to whoever is tracking him?"

"Because they were paid to do a job. We can't step on anyone's toes."

"Sam, this is not like you. What are you hiding?" Anna asked.

"Nothing. This isn't the type of suspect we can simply move on without approval. There are implications down the line that need to be considered."

"Money and government games," Anna said. "I thought we didn't play political games."

"We don't. But Demetri Andreev is a big fish. Give me ten minutes. Liberty out."

Sam disconnected the call. Anna sat at her computer reading the information scrolling rapidly across the screen. No wonder Ivan Kirch seemed too good to be true.

If she hadn't followed her hunch and had run his photo through an international database, her team would have gone to try to arrest a man known for killing his enemies.

She sent an IM to Justine and Charity so she wouldn't have to track them down in the office.

<A.Sterling>: New development in AlberTron case.
Return to the conference room for a debriefing.

Less than a minute later, Justine and Charity entered the room.

"Holy hell. I can't believe this. I know I said embezzlers were boring, but you had to dig *this* up," Justine said.

Anna was streaming information from her computer to the flat screen at the end of the conference room.

"Demetri Andreev . . . are you sure?" Justine asked.

"Yes. I've sent you the same files. The connection isn't as hazy as you'd think it would be. Once I found this link, everything kind of unfolded."

"It always does," Charity said. "So why is he working as a CFO in the US?"

"I don't know," Anna said. "And why is he taking the money from AlberTron?"

"Once a criminal, always a criminal," Justine said. "He probably thought it would be easy and no one would notice."

"I think there's more to it than that. He doesn't need the money. He makes an insane amount from his legitimate work," Charity said.

"I know," Anna said. She wasn't a good profiler, because of her own sense of justice. She had always believed someone was innately good or bad. Good followed the rules and kept the world safe, and the bad did things in that gray area. She didn't like the gray area and had never believed that one person could walk freely in that area outside the law and still be good.

Charity tapped Ivan/Demetri's picture on the screen. "When did you say Ivan first showed up in the databases?"

"Eleven years ago, why?"

"That was when his brother went to jail," Charity said. "He must have changed his identity when he realized his family wouldn't be protected if he didn't."

"What family?" Justine asked.

"His wife and kids," Anna said. It really made her mad to realize Ivan/Demetri hadn't kept his new persona clean for his family. She might have respected him a little bit if he'd created this new life and kept it legal, but instead he'd left himself vulnerable to their investigation. "Do his kids mean nothing to him?"

Justine shrugged. "I think men like him don't worry about getting caught."

"Why wouldn't he? He saw what could happen when his brother was arrested," Anna said.

"He probably thinks he's smarter or something," Charity said.

"What did Sam say?"

"That we are in a holding pattern. He needs to get clearance for us to move."

"Wow," Justine said. "If that's the case, you must have cracked someone else's mission, Anna."

Anna shrugged. She didn't think that was the entire reason Sam wanted them to wait. Her father had been an ambassador for most of his life, and Anna had learned early on that governments always had an agenda, even when dealing with criminals. There was always someone else they wanted to find. Some bigger fish they were willing to negotiate with a criminal to get to.

No matter how vile the crimes.

"Damn, girl, you look pissed off," Justine said.

Anna forced her normal, serene expression back on her face. "I'm not pissed."

"Yes, you are."

"No, I'm not. When a British woman's pissed, she's drunk, and I'm clearly not."

"Well, you're mad as hell. What's up?"

"I just don't like seeing someone like Kirch get off with a lighter sentence because we think we need information from him. I can find the same information."

"Yes, you can. But governments are looking for bigger arrests."

"Bigger than Kirch? He's a merchant of death. There

isn't an uprising in the world that Demetri Andreev hasn't supplied the weapons for—sometimes on both sides of the war."

"Sam will let us get him," Charity said. "We need to make sure we're ready to go. This isn't going to be the cakewalk I thought it would be."

"Things are never as easy as I expect them to be," Anna said. And that was the truth. She'd spent her entire life trying to make the world a better place.

"That's always been my experience, but I keep hoping life is easier for my friends," Justine said.

"Me, too," Anna said. Ivan Kirch wasn't going to know what hit him by the time she got finished with him. She couldn't tolerate men who thought they were free to act above the law. And if Sam let Ivan Kirch aka Demetri Andreev get a plea deal, she was going to be very disappointed. Oh, hell, who was she kidding? She'd be pissed—American style.

Jack Savage wasn't the kind of man who cared what anyone else thought of him. So when he got the summons to DC, his first instinct was to ignore it. The last time he was summoned to the Pentagon, he found out his superior—the man he'd given his loyalty to—had betrayed his team. Jack had had to plug the leak and clean up the mess. And Jack wasn't anyone's butler.

It had been a long day—hell, it had been a long year, and it was only February. Snow blew by the window in sideways gusts. Jack wanted nothing more than to enjoy a few days' R & R at his home on Florida's gulf coast. It was nothing more than a three-room cottage his great-grandfather had built years ago, but it was his place, more home than his fancy Arlington condo or this office had ever been.

He no longer worked for the US government. Being betrayed by his superior officer had taught him that both loyalty and justice were hard to come by. When he'd built his own team, he'd looked for other men who'd been similarly disillusioned.

They were the Savage Seven, and in most circles they were referred to as mercenaries. And Jack didn't give a shit about that. Mercenaries had been around as long as mankind had been warring . . . in other words, forever.

And he wasn't suited for any other kind of work except fighting and killing.

His team met him at the airport. They looked out of place among the tourists and business people waiting around for their flights. All his men were weapons, with instincts honed to a razor's edge.

Kirk Mann was the first to ask him about the mission. Jack suspected his expression had to match his mood, which meant he was ready to kill.

"What's the hurry?" Kirk asked. Kirk and Jack had worked together for the CIA and had saved each other's necks a time or two. He was one of the few men Jack really trusted.

"Beats me, but the client said there is no time to waste," Jack said. He didn't want to start talking about what the client had alluded to. The capture of one of the most wanted weapons dealers was something his team would want to be part of. But the information was spotty, though the fact that the client was paying them a lot of money for their services gave the client the right to be a little sketchy on the details.

"Pentagon?"

"No, not this time. A detective agency from the private sector. I'll brief everyone in the vehicle on the way."

"Yes, sir."

Though they were no longer a military unit, they functioned with the discipline of one. They were a ragged group of men who all owed their allegiance to Jack. He kept his past from the men because he didn't like explaining himself. The policy he put forth for the men was that their company would take only the best-paying assignments, which they all knew meant were the most dangerous, but these guys just didn't care.

"Where are we meeting, J.P.?" Jack asked. J.P. was the logistics expert in the team and was responsible for coordinating transportation to and from all their mission assignments.

"Out front in three," Kirk said; he was Jack's second in command. The rest of the team consisted of Harry Donovan, a munitions expert and engineer; Tommy Lazarus, communications; and Hammond—or Hamm—MacIntyre, weapons expert. The seventh of their team was Armand, who had died two years ago, and they had never replaced him. The guys weren't sure they'd trust anyone else to be in their circle.

They made their way outside to the Range Rover J.P. had secured. It was big enough to seat all of them.

It was snowing and slushy in February, and Jack cursed. He hated cold, wet weather.

Once they were all in the car and driving, Jack turned to face his men from the passenger seat. "We have a lead on Demetri Andreev."

"A solid one? The last time we went after that bastard we ended up with nothing to show for it but windburn," Hamm said.

"It's pretty damned solid," Jack said. "We're going to collect the information from the group who found him. They will be a part of the capture."

"Why the hell? We don't need any extra manpower," Kirk said.

"Because they found him, and he's been living under an alias. They were tracking him for embezzling, and they need to collar him to wrap up their case."

"Who is it? Anyone we know?"

"Liberty Investigations," Jack said.

Some of the guys nodded. Liberty Investigations had a reputation for being very good at what they did. Their paths had never crossed, but Jack had always been intrigued by what he'd heard of the team. Three women who were lethal . . . hell, it sounded very intriguing.

"Where is Andreev?"

"Seattle."

"Damn, more cold. I thought embezzlers ran to the Caribbean or some other warm, exotic place," J.P. said.

"Not all of them do. We don't all need to go to the meeting. Drop me off at the offices, and then we'll meet at the private airport where Liberty Investigations keeps their jet."

"Sounds good, boss," Kirk said. "We'll make sure everything is ready by the time you rendezvous with us."

Ten minutes later they pulled up in front of a nondescript office building, and Jack got out. He pulled up the collar of his trench coat to cover the back of his neck. He really hated the cold, but he ignored it as he walked to the door. The door was open, and he walked in. There was no receptionist. Now he faced a locked glass door.

He hit the buzzer and identified himself. The inner door unlocked, and he entered.

He wasn't too sure where to go but heard voices at the end of the hallway.

He followed them and stood in the doorway watching three really hot-looking women arguing.

"I don't think we need some rough-and-tough mercenary to do this job, Sam."

The woman who spoke had a crisp British accent and thick, dark blond hair. Her features were delicate and petite.

"Well, because you ladies haven't dealt with the Andreev clan before, and I have, I think I might be of some service," Jack said.

The blonde turned to face him, and her expression was one of outrage at his intrusion, but she quickly masked it. "And you are?"

"Jack Savage. You?"

"Anna Sterling. Contrary to what you may think, we are perfectly capable of capturing a terrorist without your assistance."

He gave her a once-over, letting his gaze drift over her slim, curvy body. He knew women were lethal—had learned that lesson the hard way—but there was something about this chick that said she hadn't spent a lot of time out of the office.

She was hot as hell and just the kind of woman he'd always wanted. But she also had a certain sophistication that made him believe she was out of his league. And he knew that shouldn't have disappointed him as much as it did.

Chapter Three

Anna was beyond annoyed that Sam had brought in mercenaries to help them collar Ivan Kirch. She'd dealt with them before, and on their last mission they'd had to renegotiate to keep the mercenary they'd hired working for them.

And this man . . . this Jack Savage . . . she had no doubt he'd chosen that name for himself to make sure he sounded like the biggest badass in the mercenary business. She realized she was clenching her hands into fists and took a deep breath.

She refused to let him know he was getting to her. She wasn't going to play mind games with Mr. Soldier of Fortune over there. Instead she was going to calmly gather her computer and the intelligence she'd uncovered and then go to her office and turn on some really loud music—probably Godsmack or Radiohead—and then she was going to scream until she felt a measure of calm.

"Thanks for getting here as quickly as you did, Jack," Sam said. "Please come in and have a seat. Anna, will you bring us all up to speed on what you've found?"

"I'd be happy to, Sam. Did you buzz Jack in?"

"Yes, I did," Sam said.

"Next time let us know we aren't alone," Justine said.

"I will. I'm sorry if it made for any uncomfortable moments."

"Didn't bother me," Jack said with what would have been a charming smile on any other man, but on him it looked like a smirk. Anna really didn't want to have to deal with him. Which wasn't like her. She usually had no problems with anyone. How could this man, that she'd just met, get under her skin? He was good-looking in a very rough way, and damn her but she'd always found that kind of tough guy attractive.

"It didn't bother me either," Anna said. "I still think some hired gun isn't necessary to finish this job."

"You might change your mind when you hear that Kirch/Andreev has left the country," Sam said.

"When?" Jack asked.

"Was he alerted to the imminent arrest?"

"Yes. Marcus called his executive staff together and told them to expect the name of the embezzler tomorrow morning. After that Andreev left the building and boarded a plane for Canada."

"Why didn't we have this information?" Justine asked.

"It's just coming through now," Anna said. She realized Sam was receiving this information as soon as they were. She tuned out the meeting and Jack and instead started working on her computer. This was where she was an expert, and she would much rather trace information through the Internet than deal with Sam right now.

There were no records of Kirch or Andreev leaving Vancouver International, but that didn't surprise Anna. He had about five active aliases. She downloaded the list she'd compiled from Interpol and other government organization databases.

"Are you running names through airline records?" Jack asked, leaning over her shoulder.

His aftershave was spicy and woodsy and altogether too yummy-smelling for him. She nodded tightly and then sent the information to the large screen at the end of the conference room so he could watch it up there.

She also tapped into a second program, one she'd started when they'd first taken the AlberTron case. It was a small tracker she'd installed in all the "new" smartphones Marcus Ware was giving his executives. To be honest, searching Andreev/Kirch's smartphone was what had given her the break she'd needed finding his real identity.

She accessed the tracking system and added that to the screen for everyone to review. "He's already on the move, it looks like across Canada."

"Yes, it does. What system is this?"

"The tracking device we put in the smartphones."

"I knew that would pay off," Charity said. "Embezzlers are always ready to run."

"Do we assume he's running because of the embezzling?" Justine asked. "And how much time do you think we have until he ditches the smartphone?"

"From his profile I'd say he's going to assume we aren't smart enough to have made the connection," Charity said.

"I'd have to agree. He seemed to think women weren't as capable of doing the job as men. Remember that comment he made?" Anna asked.

"Yes. I almost jumped over the table and punched him," Justine said.

Anna smiled at that. This was what she loved about working with her team. "We really don't need any extra help on this one, Sam."

"I think you will," Jack said.

"I don't believe I was addressing you."

"Yeah, I know. But because we know Andreev is heading out of the country, and your team is going to have to wait for him to land before you know where he's going . . ."

"Are you trying to imply you know where he's going?" Anna asked. She really didn't like this man.

"Not imply. Andreev always heads back to Algeria when he needs to regroup. It's a land and government he's familiar with, and he has no problem disappearing there."

"Sam, why don't we have this intelligence?" Charity asked.

Anna was already running the information on her laptop. It seemed that since they'd uncovered the embezzler, everything was going at breakneck speed. Which was exactly what they liked. Sitting around waiting for things to pop made them all crazy.

But Sam should have passed this information on to them. Anna added it to a growing list of concerns in her mind about her boss. Why was he suddenly holding out on them?

Jack had never worked with a team made up of all women before, and, to be fair, he wasn't sure he liked it. He was used to men. He'd grown up with only his old man and an older brother. He'd gone into the military as soon as he was old enough and qualified for special ops where, frankly, there weren't a lot of women.

He dated some, mostly just to get laid and because he didn't want to go to a prostitute. To be honest, he didn't like paying for sex. But he didn't want a long-term commitment and rarely spent more than one night with the same woman.

So as he approached five hours of being in the same conference room with the three women, he was ready for some testosterone. He sort of counted Sam as a guy, but Sam wasn't in the office, and this team was self-managed. They weren't looking for a man's guidance, and Jack was impressed at how well they worked together.

He could use someone like Anna on his team. Though his communications expert was good, he didn't have the magic touch Anna had with computers. When any of them mentioned a location or a resource, she had the information in moments.

Charity, Justine, and Anna reminded Jack a little of his team. And he saw a few things he'd like to integrate into the way the Savage Seven—Six—worked.

"Are your men going to be ready when we are?" Anna asked. She hadn't softened in the least toward him, which was understandable.

His hard-on for her hadn't softened either. He wanted her with an intense desire that took him by surprise. She was nothing like the women he usually spent time with. He would have liked to play it off as nothing more than a sexual itch, but as she wasn't his usual type of lay, he knew it was more. She was exactly the type of woman he'd always wanted.

Which made him uncomfortable, so he tried desperately to ignore the images in his head of her naked in that big leather chair.

"Jack? I asked you a question," she said, her British accent even sharper than it had been earlier.

"My men are always ready," he said. He was trying to give her a little extra room because he would be pissed as hell if his client had suddenly brought in a new team for them to have to work with.

"Wonderful. Do you require anything from me so they have the mission specs?"

"I will forward Tommy Lazarus, our comm expert, the information you've compiled. And I'll ask him to send you what we have. I think most of it you already know, but Andreev's local hangouts in Algiers might not be familiar to you."

"We haven't taken any jobs in Algeria. We tend to work for dignitaries and executives, and that country isn't exactly welcoming to foreigners," Anna said.

"Very true. We can get you up to speed on the country very quickly," Jack said, surprised she'd admitted to not knowing everything.

"I know the White City," she said carefully. Her accent wasn't as sharp, and neither was her tone. And an emotion he couldn't define passed behind her eyes.

"All the better," Jack said, trying to keep things light and focused on the mission. He didn't need to know why she'd suddenly turned pale when she'd mentioned the White City . . . well, he didn't need to know unless it would affect the mission and his team.

"When were you last in Algiers?" he asked, trusting his instincts.

"A lifetime ago," she said and glanced away as Charity walked over to them.

He wanted to say the hell with all the other women in the room and pull Anna away so he could find out more about what made her tick.

Damn, it was a very good thing Kirk wasn't there, or he'd be giving Jack hell about not focusing on the mission. Never had Jack been tempted to put anything or anyone in front of a mission.

"Jack, can you give me a minute?" Charity asked. "I need you to show us on the map the different locations Andreev's known to frequent."

Jack stood up and went to the computerized whiteboard that lined another wall. Charity called up a map of Africa.

"We can't enter through Morocco, because that border is closed. I have contacts to help us enter through Tunisia."

"That's okay, Sam will get us through in the most expedient way. It's nice to know Andreev won't have the same advantages," Justine said.

"But Andreev will more than likely go through Morocco and the mountains," Jack said.

"That is true," Anna said. "We have to remember to think like a criminal if we're going to catch him."

She looked right at him as she made that comment, and Jack realized Anna Sterling didn't like him or what he did. That pissed him off because he knew he was a necessary evil. The world they lived in was violent and turbulent, and there was always a need for a soldier-for-hire.

"I'm not a criminal," Jack said carefully. "My men are highly trained, and we do a job no one else will do. And your boss doesn't think you're familiar enough with Algeria to go in on your own," Jack said.

"I didn't mean to imply I thought you were a criminal," Anna said, looking straight through him. She turned away. "I'm almost done here."

"Good. I'm going to the airport unless you need me here. I want to check out Jack's team," Justine said.

"I'll let them know to expect you," Jack said.

"Hold up, I'll go with you," Charity said. "Anna, you get all the info from Jack and put it in one big file. Then we'll meet you at the airport."

Jack left the room while the women wrapped up whatever details they needed to. He didn't really like the idea of bringing three new people onto his team, but he did like the thought of spending more time with Anna Sterling.

She was a firecracker and a half, and that attitude of hers was enough to make him want to do something to shock her and force her out of the polite manners she retreated behind.

Anna wasn't one of those women who showed her temper through words. She didn't like to allow anyone to see that side of her. So she needed to get out of the conference room and away from Jack Savage before she broke her own personal rule.

She tried to be objective, but she really hated people who lived in the gray area of right and wrong. And working with Jack and his team wasn't going to be easy for her. Jack's mobile rang, and he stepped out of the conference room to answer it.

"Sam?"

"Yes, Anna."

"I don't think we need Savage and his team on this. Justine, Charity, and I really work better on our own."

"Normally that's true. But as soon as we uncovered the connection between Kirch and Andreev, the game changed."

"I am aware of that. But I still think we can handle this on our own. We can use Savage and his men if we need them."

"Normally I'd agree with you. But Algeria is not your normal mission spec. I think having Jack and his team on the mission will you give you the advantage you need."

"I'm not trying to be difficult, Sam."

"I know that. Are you sure you'll be okay in Algiers?" Sam asked.

"Fine. I don't let anything from my personal sphere spill over into my work sphere."

"You *are* very good at compartmentalizing," Sam said.

"That doesn't sound like a compliment."

"I was simply stating a fact. You're a bit prickly today."

"I am. I don't know why."

"Is it the mission?"

"No. I'm glad we have some action. I think I need to get out of this office, and I know Charity and Justine do."

"Good. Keep me posted," Sam said.

"I will."

Sam signed off, and Anna tried to change her mental attitude. She had some personal baggage with mercenaries from her childhood. And she didn't trust men who sold their allegiance. She didn't know what kind of man Jack was. . . .

"Except that he's a savage," she said out loud to herself.

"I *am* a Savage," Jack said.

She glanced over her shoulder. He was standing behind her looking every inch the tough-ass. She really had a chance to look at him and realized the scars and short military haircut on him weren't just part of his past, they were who he was.

"Better to be a savage than someone who spends her time hiding behind her computer."

"I don't hide behind it. I'm rated a marksmen in handguns. I have a black belt in three different martial-arts disciplines, and I am more than capable of taking on you or any other opponent."

"Then you must know the world isn't black and white. And that men like me fill a need."

"I do know that. But that doesn't mean . . . I want to say this the right way. Jack, you could be so much more. When we were planning our strategy for entering Algeria and for capturing Andreev, I heard a real intelligence in your voice."

"Why, thank you, ma'am," he said in a self-deprecating tone.

"I didn't mean it like that."

"Then how did you mean it?" he asked, moving closer to her.

"I meant you don't have to sell your gun to the highest bidder to earn a living."

He stopped next to the chair she was sitting in and leaned his hip against the arm of the chair. He was all muscle—man the way he was supposed to be when he was honed to the top of his physical best. Jack Savage was the ultimate weapon. He was smart and savvy, and Anna had no doubt he knew how to use his body to the utmost advantage on the field.

"I fill a need in this world. If my team wasn't around to take the jobs we do, people like Andreev would be supplying weapons to untrained rebels, and the killing would go on for a much longer time, Ms. Sterling."

"I'm not arguing that you're a necessary evil, Savage, I'm just saying . . . that loyalty should mean more than a dollar sign."

"Your clients could say the same of you and your teammates."

"Touché," she said. She knew better than to judge anyone by their actions. Jack wasn't a mercenary from her past. So why was she trying so hard to build a barrier between them?

She looked into his sky-blue eyes and saw the pain in them. She saw his keen intelligence and the wall he kept between himself and the world. And she felt an answering tug in her own soul.

Jack Savage was the kind of man Anna secretly wanted for her own. The kind of man who lived outside of the law and set his own standards.

He was everything she wasn't. Everything her life had always pointed her away from. He lived and breathed in that gray area between right and wrong. It wasn't necessarily the area between criminals and law-abiding citizens . . . it was an area she liked to think of as justice. She knew justice didn't always come with a badge or in a courtroom. And she saw in Jack's eyes that he knew this, too.

His life had shaped him into the kind of man who'd be more than happy to get justice for himself and his client however it had to be achieved. And if that meant working outside of the normal boundaries of the law, so be it.

"Why are you staring at me like that?" he asked. His voice was deep and rough, just another thing about him that showed her he wasn't civilized.

"I don't know," she said and then stood up and walked away before she did something really stupid like kiss him. Because giving in to a bad boy like Jack Savage was something she'd never really been tempted to do before.

But Jack Savage was temptation incarnate for her. He made her wish she was a different kind of woman so she could spend all her time with him.

Anna knew she needed to keep her mind on the mission. On making sure Demetri Andreev was captured and put out of business for good. But she couldn't help watching Jack, and he wouldn't leave her thoughts alone.

No matter how many times she tried to convince herself she didn't care what he did, she kept finding her attention drawn back to him.

She wanted him. *Oh, my God*, she thought. She was in lust for the first time in her life, and a part of her was very much afraid she was going to act on the impulse.

Chapter Four

Jack followed Anna out of the room. There was so much more to her than her sexy good looks. The more he talked to her, the more attracted to her he was. He followed her down the hall and into her office. Charity and Justine had left, so they were alone in the building.

"Anna?"

"Yes?" she said, half turning toward him.

Now that he had her attention, he didn't hesitate. He knew what he wanted from her and closed the gap between them. He touched her soft long hair, letting the cool strands flow over his fingers. She stood stock-still just watching him with those wide eyes of hers.

Her lips parted when he brushed one rough, scarred finger against the side of her face. He saw then the differences between them. Saw her pale, perfect skin and his rough, work-hardened fingers. He had calluses on his hands that would never go away.

And even though they worked in the same industry, they'd never really be in the same league. What the hell was he thinking?

He couldn't kiss Anna Sterling or even strip her naked and take her the way he wanted to. They were working together, and she was fragile for some reason when Algiers was mentioned.

He needed to pull back.

Yet as he dropped the strands of her hair, he didn't want to. So instead of pulling away, he cupped the back of her head and drew her closer to him. She leaned toward him, lifting on her tiptoes as he lowered his head.

She inhaled sharply as he brushed his lips over hers. The sweetness of her breath washed over him. She smelled clean and exotic like the flowers that grew in the verdant jungles of South America. And as his lips brushed over hers, he knew this was a big mistake.

But he didn't stop. Couldn't pull back from her.

Her lips parted, and her hands came up to his shoulders. She clutched at him, drawing him nearer as her tongue tangled with his, thrusting deep to the back of his mouth.

The kiss was deep and dirty and nothing he'd expected from the ultra-civilized Anna Sterling, yet at the same time it was exactly what he needed from her.

He wrapped his arms around her body, sent his hands down her back to hold her tightly to him. She canted her hips toward his, her center rubbing over his hard-on. He groaned deep in his throat.

Yeah, baby, he thought, *that's it. Show me you need me.*

And she rubbed her hips over him. Her breasts brushed against his chest, and he realized Anna really was a firecracker, and he wanted all of her. He wanted to use the passion between them to peel back the layers she used to hide from most of the people in the world.

And though a mission was the last place he should be thinking about seduction and sex, he knew Anna Sterling was going to be his.

He lifted his head, and her eyes opened. She was completely bare to him in that moment. There was a freshness to Anna he had never experienced with any woman before.

He cupped her face in his hands, rubbing his thumbs down her cheekbones and then scraping one thumb over her lower lip. She sucked his thumb into her mouth and looked up at him.

There was something very flirty in her reaction, and he felt it all the way to the core of his being.

"Well, that answers my question."

She tipped her head to the side. "What question?"

"If you were the woman I thought you were."

She shook her head and backed away from him. "I'm not like that. . . . I mean, normally I'm not a very passionate person. I think you're making me . . ." She wrapped one arm around her waist and took a step back and bumped into her desk. "That's not true. You aren't making me do anything, but you do tempt me, Jack Savage."

"I do?"

She punched him in the arm. "Don't be a smartass."

He laughed because despite the dangerous mission they were about to go on, he liked her. He was happy with the thought of spending time with her. Especially in his world—a place to which he'd never taken a woman before. And that scared him a little.

So he dropped back into the role he wasn't scared to fill: tactical leader. He'd put them back on the business track and wait until they were alone again to explore this attraction.

He knew himself well enough to know that nothing would stop him from having her, even the knowledge that Anna wasn't the type of woman he normally confined himself to. He couldn't fool himself into thinking he was a great catch, but he knew Anna was the type of woman who wouldn't give herself lightly to any man.

"We need to head out. My team will be anxious to get in the air," Jack said.

She blinked at him. "Of course. You can wait for me in the inner lobby. I just need to gather my stuff, and I'll be ready to go."

"I'll wait here," he said.

"I'm sorry if that sounded like an optional request, but I need a few minutes alone."

"Why?" he asked.

"Because I do."

"I'm not leaving," he said. "I like being with you."

"Then why did you just change the subject to business? Why not spend a few minutes just enjoying each other?" she asked.

He shrugged. "I'm not really much more than a savage."

"You're a lot more than that, but I think you've gotten used to just sticking to that one role."

The ride to the corporate airport, where the Liberty Investigations jet was kept, was silent. Jack didn't mind silence. He kept his attention on the road in front of him, and Anna kept hers fixed to the BlackBerry in her hand.

She had started reading e-mails and texting her teammates as soon as they'd gotten into the car. He'd allowed her to ignore him because he wasn't really in the mood for talking.

Being attracted to her was a distraction, and he truly knew he couldn't afford that. He tried to let the cold February weather seep into his bones and cool off his libido, but it didn't work. Instead he pictured Anna lying in his arms in front of the fireplace in his small Florida home.

What the hell?

He'd never brought any woman there and doubted Anna would ever see it either.

"The turn is just up there on the right," she said.

"Thanks. Did you get the information from Tommy?"

"Yes. Thank you for having him send it. I added it to the database I have, and we can start triangulating where Andreev is. The tracker in his smartphone is still working."

"Good. I think he'll probably ditch the phone in either France or Morocco, but if he keeps it, that will give us an advantage," Jack said. He wasn't used to talking with women, and he knew this put him at a disadvantage with her.

"I think we're going to land in the airport outside of Algiers," Anna said.

"Yes, we are. When were you there last?" he asked.

"As a teenager. My father was the British ambassador to Algeria."

"Did you move around a lot as a kid?" he asked. He tried to guess her age and figured her for early thirties. She would have been in Algeria in the early nineties, when there was a lot of political unrest.

"We moved a fair amount. My brother and I liked it a lot when we were little."

"What did you like about it?" he asked.

"The new cultures and people. But after a while I started to realize that for all the differences of the cultures we visited, there was a sameness to life everywhere."

Jack glanced over at her. "I've found that, too. Wherever I've traveled for my job, I'm struck by the universal truth of all societies. There's rich and poor, there's arrogant and hungry, and there is always someone who wants more power."

"I would think the sameness you see comes from going to places on the cusp of anarchy."

"It's not always anarchy. Sometimes it's genocide or things like one government's need to control something they have no rights to."

"Like oil?"

Jack nodded. "I was in Special Forces before getting out and starting my own group."

"Why did you do that?"

"I needed the freedom to make my own choices and not worry so much about the government's agenda. I've seen my country leave men behind to die because to rescue them would mean admitting we were someplace we weren't supposed to be."

Anna just looked at him.

"I know that makes me sound bitter, and I guess a part of me is, but another part just knows that's the way of government negotiations and the way of the world."

She nodded. "I've seen that, too. I was kidnapped when we were in Algeria because one terror group didn't like the British foreign policy in the Middle East. My father was torn between being my dad and wanting my safety and being the British government's representative. He couldn't give in to terrorist demands, but . . . it was hard for him. And as a child I didn't get it, really, but now as an adult I do."

Jack pulled into a parking spot outside of the hangar where the Liberty Investigations jet was waiting. He left the car running and turned toward Anna. Some of the mystery he'd sensed in her was starting to make sense—the barriers she kept between herself and the world. "I had no idea."

"Why would you? Most of the world never knew what happened. And my name was never released. I didn't tell you to gain sympathy, just to show you I really do understand that the needs of one can't be outweighed by the needs of many."

Jack was humbled by what she'd said. But he also now understood her position on right and wrong and the vehemence he'd heard in her tone when she'd talked about him selling his honor to the highest bidder. "Were you taken captive by a group of mercenaries?"

She nodded. "I don't talk about that."

"Fair enough," he said. "But don't judge me or my men by the other mercenaries you've met in the past."

"Why not?"

"Because we aren't like those men."

"Really? What makes you different?"

"A kind of sacrifice you won't be able to understand," he said, thinking of all the things his men had lost. Some of them had lost innocence, others family, others their faith in anything other than themselves. And he knew if Anna treated them the way she'd treated him, some of the men—like Kirk—would make it very difficult for them to work together.

"I don't need social advice from you, Jack. I've been interacting with all kinds of people for years."

He leaned over and grabbed the back of her neck. He hated that haughty tone of hers. The one that said *I'm better than you.*

He kissed her hard and deep, thrusting his tongue into her mouth. She drew back and looked up at him. "Don't do that again."

"I'll do whatever I damn well please, Anna Sterling, and you had best remember that."

"Don't act like a prick, Jack Savage, or I'll show you you have a lot more to fear than you think you do."

He shook his head. There was no give in this girl, and as much as that turned him on, he knew it could spell trouble for them down the road.

Anna got out of the vehicle, glad to no longer be alone with Jack. She didn't like the way she was acting around him. For years no one had shaken her facade of normalcy, and now this man was getting to her. Making her question things she'd buried in the past. Things she wanted—no, needed—to leave there. Yet she couldn't.

"Hey, girl. Where's the fire?" Justine said as Anna entered the hangar.

"There's no fire, I just want to get to Algeria, find Andreev, and bring him to justice."

"Me, too. I can't believe that slimy bastard got away."

"Me neither," Charity said as she joined them. Standing near the cargo hold of the plane were a group of five men.

Anna watched out of her periphery as Jack joined his group. They were almost silent as they worked. She saw them talking, but it was quiet. She knew they had to be the best in the business because Sam wouldn't ask them to work with a group that would sell them out.

Liberty Investigations had all learned a hard lesson when Piper had been kidnapped. And trusting the wrong person could get them killed.

"You looked really pissed off," Justine said.

She wasn't pissed off, she was just . . . agitated. How could one man do this to her? "I am not. I have the new information from one of the Savage team with known hangouts for Andreev. I e-mailed them to both of you."

"We got it. I've been talking to Hamm. He used to be army. I think most of Savage's team is ex-military, and they seem to have a strong sense of patriotism," Charity said.

"I'll start running background checks on the men once we're in the air. That way we won't have any surprises."

"Good idea," Justine said. "They look like decent guys, but appearances can be deceiving."

Justine had a long history of not trusting any men, especially those who seemed to be good guys on the surface. Anna realized the situation with Jack's team could be very tense, given Justine's attitude. She knew she'd have to keep her own distrust of mercenaries to herself.

"Sam sent me a message saying Marcus Ware will pay for all our expenses. He wants Kirch/Andreev caught and brought back to the States for trial," Charity said.

"I don't know if we're going to get him alive," Justine said. "He's not going to want to end up in prison like his brother."

"That was my thought, too. Andreev isn't going to go down without a big fight. What kind of weapons did you bring?" Anna asked.

"I got everything I thought we could use, and I upgraded our body armor. Andreev will have cutting-edge technology. I want to know what he's selling so we have an idea of what he'll have. I know he has armor-piercing bullets. Can you find out what else?" Justine asked. Justine always made sure they had enough weapons and ammo on a mission.

Though they all carried their own handguns and spare clips, there was always a need for more weapons. Justine also made sure they had the tiny two-way radios they used to communicate with each other when their BlackBerry smartphones weren't usable.

"Justine, do you know if they're using the same communications tools we are?" Charity asked.

"I think so. I talked to Lazarus, and we did a quick test. I think integrating our teams' communications will be easy to do. I'm not sure how well either of us is going to be able to work with each other, however. They're pretty much used to just working with men. And I know none of us are that keen on dealing with so much testosterone."

Anna had to laugh at the way Justine had said that. It was true, though. The three of them worked well together because they were all similar deep inside. They didn't trust easily, they never gave up, and they all knew they were the very best at what they did.

"We'll figure it out as we go along. I think it will be better to divide up mission objectives so we each work separately," Anna said.

"That won't work," Jack said, coming up behind her.

Anna noticed he had three of his men with him. He fourth was still at the rear of the plane on his mobile.

"It was just a thought. Hello, boys, I'm Anna Sterling," she said, introducing herself to the men.

"This is Hamm MacIntyre, J.P. Fields, and Harry Donovan," Jack said. "Over in the corner on the cell phone is Kirk Mann, and the man talking to the pilot is Tommy Lazarus."

"Nice to meet you all," Anna said.

They all nodded. "I think we're ready to get in the air. We can discuss the op in the plane."

"I agree," Charity said.

Anna listened to the conversation with half an ear while she typed in the names of Jack's team members. She sent a message to Sam from her BlackBerry and asked him to confirm the spellings.

Sam confirmed it and sent her a file with the information he'd used to make the decision to hire the Savage Seven. But Jack had introduced only six men, she thought.

"Who's the seventh in your group?" she asked when the conversation around her ebbed. All the men stopped and looked at her. It was unnerving to have that much attention trained at her at one moment.

Jack finally said, "Armand Mitterand. He was killed a little over a year ago."

"I'm sorry you lost one of your team," Anna said. "Why haven't you changed your name or replaced him?"

"Because he's irreplaceable," J.P. said. "He was one of a kind. And we kept the name to honor him."

Anna nodded. She realized these men were all a bit like

Jack. Rough around the edges and loyal, it seemed, at least to each other.

What that meant for this mission and them working together, she wasn't sure, but she added Armand's name to her list. By the time they landed in Europe for refueling, she'd have answers to most of her questions.

She only wished she could as easily figure out the new feelings she had for Jack Savage. But men were something she'd never understood. And men like Jack . . . well, she freely admitted she'd never really met a man like Jack before.

Maybe that was why he was throwing her for a loop. She had no way of knowing who he really was or, for that matter, what she wanted from him.

Lust was easy and not really worth this much angst, but she knew she wanted more from Jack than his body. She wanted . . . Oh, damn, she wanted him to be the man she kept getting glimpses of.

The man who could be so much more than a savage. The man who could wake her up inside.

Chapter Five

Jack and his men were tense on the flight to Algiers. Because of diplomatic problems, they'd have to land in Morrocco and illegally cross the border. That wasn't a problem for his men—they were used to flying under the radar. But the women of Liberty Investigations didn't seem like they could go anywhere unnoticed.

He wondered who Sam Liberty was that he would assemble three totally hot women to kick ass. There was a certain diabolical madness to that thought. That he'd find women who didn't look like they'd ever done anything harder than apply their lip gloss and train them to be lethal weapons. . . .

Yet the masculine part of him couldn't believe the women were truly weapons. Especially Anna. He'd held her in his arms, and that had screwed up his thinking because now when he looked at her he saw sex bunny instead of trained operative.

The petite Justine wasn't as deceptive as the supermodel Charity. There was menace in Justine's eyes that belied the dark-haired, pixie-featured sweetness of her appearance.

"If you're planning to charm your way through our team, I have to warn you Charity isn't available."

"For what?" Jack said, glancing up at Anna as she slid onto the padded seat next to him.

Anna leaned around him, blocking his view of the other woman. Her long blond hair swung forward, and he inhaled the sweet floral scent of her.

"For dating. She's engaged," Anna said.

"Thanks for the info," he said, pitching his voice low so it didn't carry further than Anna. "But I'm not interested in her."

"Then why are you staring at her the way a starving man stares at a steak?" she asked, arching one eyebrow at him.

"Why do you care?" he asked.

She shrugged, the motion delicate and feminine, and he knew he was out of his element with this woman. He had no business flirting with her, none at all. But he'd be damned if he was going to stop.

"I don't," she said. Then she looked him straight in the eye. "That's not true. I care because I can tell you are distracted, and in our line of work distracted leads to mistakes, and mistakes are costly."

"I am distracted, Ms. Sterling, but not by Charity or Justine. I'm distracted because I've spent my entire life working with men, and I have no idea if you women are going to be able to keep up."

Her eyes narrowed. "You're too good at this not to have done your research."

He shook his head. "That's the distracting part. I do know what the three of you are capable of. I've heard the stories and read the mission recaps Sam forwarded to me, but I can't reconcile that information with what I see."

She leaned back in the seat, crossing her arms under her breasts. She was wearing a very refined, conservative blouse that buttoned down the front. It was feminine but not sexy at all, so there was no reason for him to suddenly need to adjust his legs to make room for his erection.

That little gap between the buttons of her blouse wasn't meant to entice him, but he was enticed nonetheless. There was an innate sexiness to every move Anna Sterling made, and nothing he did to resist her made a difference. He wanted her.

"That makes no sense," she said. "Your guys—"

"It's a totally different kettle of fish," he said. "Men are expected to be tough-asses."

"They are? Where is that written?"

"It's not a law or rule of thumb, Anna," he said. He liked her name and the way it sounded on his lips.

"What is it, then?" she asked, her voice softer now, not combative like it had been before. She leaned a bit closer to him, and it was all he could do not to reach out and touch her.

He wanted to caress the softness of her skin and just let that feeling sink in to him. He'd never had a soft life, and yet it was something he sometimes craved.

"It's instinct. Men have been protecting their communities since the dawn of time."

She shook her head. "Women have been doing the very same thing, just in a different way."

"That's my point. If you told me you'd be keeping the home fires burning, I'd get that, but your team is telling me you're going to ride shotgun, and I know you're capable of doing that, but my brain is saying, 'Hey, buddy, that's not right.' "

She smiled at him. "That's chauvinism. I'm not sure if you got the memo or not, but it's dead."

"I must have missed that one. In the places where I've been, it's not dead."

"Well, I'll just have to make sure you change your thinking."

"How are you going to do that?"

She shrugged delicately. "I think I'll keep my plan to myself for now."

"You do that," he said, leaning over. He wanted to kiss that sassy mouth of hers.

"Savage," Kirk said.

He turned away from Anna and glanced toward the middle of the plane where his guys were all seated. Kirk was frowning at him. And it didn't take a genius to figure out that Kirk thought he was distracted.

Fuck it, he thought. Anna Sterling was more than a distraction, and he needed his head in the game. They'd been tracking Andreev for more years than he wanted to count. The man was one of the most dangerous in the world. A merchant of death who sold his weapons to whomever had the money, sometimes prolonging conflicts by years and adding to the death count in places where genocide and rebellion were the standard.

Jack pushed to his feet and walked to to his men. He needed to remember where he belonged, and it wasn't next to the softness that was Anna.

"I don't like this," Justine said as Anna joined her and Charity at the front of the plane. The Liberty Investigations jet had a desk area in the front of the plane, a general sitting area toward the middle—where the Savage Seven were camped out—and a bedroom/shower suite in the back.

"What don't you like?" Anna asked.

"Them," Justine said. "There's just something unsettling about all those men on our plane."

Anna agreed to a certain extent, but if it weren't for her

distracting attraction to Jack Savage, she'd almost like having the other men around. They were changing the dynamic of her team. Making her and the others more of a unit than they had been for the last two assignments.

She missed her friends, and while she didn't begrudge them their newfound relationships, there was a part of her that had feared their team would never be the same again.

"It *is* different, isn't it?" Anna asked.

"Change is good," Charity said.

"I guess," Justine said. She was grumpy by nature and didn't necessarily like a lot of men.

Anna's BlackBerry beeped, and she glanced down at the screen to see that the program she'd written to notify her of Andreev's moves was alerting her.

"Be right back," she said and went to her desk. She sat down and pulled up the program.

Given the jump start Andreev had on them, she expected to find his signal in North Africa. But instead she noticed the cell phone she'd bugged had stopped in Paris.

"What'd you find?" Charity asked.

"Andreev's stopped moving. His signal is in Paris," Anna said. She started typing to pinpoint his exact location. Jack and his second in command, Kirk, walked over to her desk.

Anna didn't look up but kept her fingers moving on the keyboard.

"He stopped at Charles de Gaulle. I'm not sure what terminal he's in," she said—really to herself.

"Can you access the airport security cameras?" Kirk asked.

"Yes," she said. She ignored the others as Hamm, too, joined them. She accessed the airport security system using a master code all international security people used.

"Can one of you find me the flight numbers that have just landed and which one he might be on?"

"I'm on it," Kirk said.

She accessed the CCTV system and pulled up the multi-camera view. It was complex, and it took her a moment to orient herself with the airport she'd flown in and out of many times during her life. Finally she identified terminals one, two, and three. Terminal one was undergoing major construction right now, so she minimized those windows. She wished she'd put the GPS tracker on Andreev's smartphone. Ticked off at herself for not thinking of adding that feature, she was determined to find Andreev and apprehend him before he got to Africa, if they could.

"Justine, contact Sam and see if we have any operatives at Charles de Gaulle. Maybe we can nab Andreev there. . . ."

"I'm on it."

"There are two flights he might be on," Kirk said, "They both landed in terminal two. One is Air France flight AF49, which is in terminal two-A. The other is a Delta flight Air France. . . . Never mind, they're the same flight. So it should be two-A."

Anna zoomed in on the terminal Kirk had indicated and Jack crowded in behind her on the left as Charity moved in on the right. Anna could see the passengers disembarking from the flight Kirk had indicated.

She hit a button to record the video they were streaming and then maximized the window so she could zoom in on the passengers. Charity held next to the screen a photo of Andreev as they'd last seen him.

Anna felt the tension in everyone as they watched, searching though the crowd. She didn't see anyone who fit Andreev's body image. She didn't bother searching for someone who had his looks. Andreev hadn't evaded capture as long as he had by being stupid, so she knew he'd have a disguise.

"I wish we knew how he moved," Charity said.

"Me, too. I can't quite figure out if that was him or not."

"Where?" Jack asked.

Anna pointed. He was huskier than Andreev had been when they'd seen him last.

Jack put his hand on the desk next to hers and leaned over her. His body heat wrapped around her, and for a moment she closed her eyes to try to deal with the dizzying sensation of Jack.

"I'm not sure. We have some film of him from eighteen months ago that's kind of grainy. We can compare it."

She nodded, and he leaned back.

The new dynamic isn't working, she thought. *Jack is too much of a distraction.* It didn't matter that he was making Anna and Charity and Justine up their game at the same time that this stupid attraction was making her crazy.

She'd never been distracted by a man before. Why him?

"Anna?"

"Yes?"

"I said Sam has two agents at the airport. Just send them the video clip, and they'll detain whomever we identify," Justine said.

"I'm on it." She forwarded the clip. "Anyone else?"

"I thought this guy looks a bit like him," Charity said.

Anna sent the next clip to Sam, and then she looked at Jack.

"You're going to think I'm crazy but . . . that woman," he said.

She watched the movements of the woman and had to agree that something wasn't right with the way she was moving. Anna sent it on to Sam.

"Now we wait. And watch the tracking signal."

Anna sat back in her chair, realizing she might have been wrong about Jack and his team. They were actually good to work with, and though she'd never find it easy to trust mercenaries, she was starting to trust them.

And that didn't bother her as much as she thought it should.

* * *

Sam's agents detained and interviewed all three suspects, and none of them were Andreev, which was frustrating not just to Jack but to the entire team. His men were on edge, unused to inactivity or the quiet background chatter of the women.

They usually used the travel time to a mission to build up their aggression. They bonded by slinging insults and curses at each other, and usually there was at least one bare-knuckled fight on the flights.

But the presence of the women was keeping his men in check. And Jack wasn't sure how long it would be before one of his guys went off.

Anna signaled him, and he left his spot in the plane to go to her.

"We've lost the signal on Andreev's phone. I think he ditched it," Anna said. "Charity is tracking private-plane and commercial flights from Paris to see if we can pinpoint where he'll land. We still think Morocco is the best bet, and we'll be going with that."

"When did you decide all this? This is a joint venture."

"I'm aware of that. We just got the news and made the decision. If you want us to drop you somewhere else, we can do that," Anna said in that haughty tone that set his nerves on fire.

"Because our mission objective is two-fold, I don't think that option is going to work."

"Two-fold?"

"Sam hired us to apprehend Andreev and to keep you girls safe."

She crossed her arms over her chest. "Girls?"

"Girls. Now, I need to talk to my men," he said, walking away before he did something stupid like kiss her again.

Jack wasn't too surprised that they'd lost the tracking signal. Andreev had survived for a long time, and so far the only mistake he'd made was the embezzling thing. He wondered why Andreev had done it.

"What was that about?" Kirk asked, stopping Jack before he reached the rest of the team.

"Andreev ditched the cell phone. We need to work our contacts and see if he's still heading back to his base in Algiers. Do you still have your contacts?"

"Yeah, I'll go see what I can find out," Kirk said, but he made no move to leave.

"What?"

Kirk rubbed the back of his neck. "The guys and I have been talking. . . . We need to be operating on our own. Let the Liberty Investigations team go to France and follow the leads there."

"Well, it's not up for a vote," Jack said.

Kirk stared back at him. "For Christ's sake, Jack, you're acting like a horny fool who's thinking about getting laid. We don't work with another team. And those girls might be good in the corporate world or acting as snipers, but Andreev is a different kettle of fish. And the Jack I know would agree with my assessment."

"Are you questioning my judgment?"

Kirk shook his head and turned away but turned back. "Yeah, I guess I am. Something's not right with you now. Why is that?"

"Maybe because we're going after the one guy who's eluded us for so long. The one guy we all have a score to settle with."

Kirk nodded. "I'll give you that."

Jack was the leader, and the group wasn't a democracy. The only way this team worked and thrived was through his leadership. They needed to know who was in charge, and the leader—he—could show no weakness.

He briefed his team on the latest, but Kirk still was restless and kept making comments under his breath. Finally Jack pushed to his feet and got in Kirk's face.

"You have a problem with me, Kirk?"

Kirk stretched his arms out in front of him and pushed Jack back. "I don't like the way you keep talking with Anna."

"We're working with her team."

"Yeah, but the look on your face says you have more than just teamwork on your mind."

"Again, is that a problem?" Jack didn't want to have this conversation in front of all his men.

"It could be. Men who are distracted are dead."

"I know that better than anyone here," Jack said.

The other men just sat between him and Kirk, quiet, tense, waiting. Jack didn't know if he was going to have to fight this out with Kirk or not. Physicality was the one language his guys always understood.

"I think Kirk is just saying we want Andreev, and letting him slip through our fingers again isn't something we're going to let happen," Hamm said.

"I'm not about to. What's up, guys? Suddenly you don't trust me?"

Hamm shook his head. "It's not that. We've just never seen you lose focus before. You want to chase a piece of tail, fine. But we're not willing to die so you can get lucky."

Jack grabbed Hamm by the shirtfront and drew him to his feet. "Never question my leadership unless you are willing to back it up."

"I'm willing, you son of a bitch," Kirk said, grabbing Jack's arm and throwing a punch at his jaw.

Jack responded with a punch to Hamm's gut that dropped Hamm back in his seat. The tension exploded around him as Jack and Kirk slugged it out. Jack used the fight to clear his head until they were both bloody and Kirk was forced on his ass. Jack glanced around at his men.

"Do I really seem like I've changed?"

All the men muttered no and went back to checking their weapons. The tension on his team had dissipated.

Jack had needed the fight as much as Kirk had. The guys were used to cursing and acting like men, but with the woman around they were trapped in the manners that had been drilled into them since they'd entered boot camp.

Even Jack had a hard time letting go with the women around. They were changing the dynamic of his team. And he knew it was a new world and one that they had to get used to.

Women could do just about any job these days, but that didn't mean men were ready for it.

Well, not all men, he thought. But he wondered if he'd ever really be able to accept the fact that a woman like Anna could defend herself. He had spent a lifetime protecting people he didn't know, and now that he'd found a woman he wanted to protect . . . she didn't need him for that.

Chapter Six

"Can I talk to you?" Anna said, taking Jack by the hand and drawing him through the sprawled knot of his men toward the bedroom at the back of the plane.

She heard Charity offering first aid to Kirk, who had a broken nose and bloodied lip. Jack didn't look much better. Anna was angry at herself for thinking he was more than the savage he seemed.

Justine had said that men just needed time to settle things between themselves, and, to be honest, Anna knew that, but Jack's team operated at a level above hers. And physically kicking your own team member's ass wasn't something she understood.

She was angry at Jack for not being the man she'd been hoping he would be. But she wasn't surprised. Deep inside she knew that any man who looked and acted the way he did was a savage.

She let go of him once they were in the bedroom, and she closed the door. "Have a seat."

"I'll stand, thanks," he said, wiping his hand over the back of his lip.

"What was that about?"

"A little matter needed to be settled."

"And talking wouldn't work?" she asked.

"Nope," he said, walking around her to the bathroom. She watched him wash his face and realized she had no idea why she'd brought him in here, except . . .

No idea. . . .

"I don't understand you."

"Maybe you aren't supposed to."

"Jack, don't be more difficult than you already are."

"Am I?"

"Yes, you are. Why didn't you just talk to Kirk or let him think about whatever was between you two?"

"Sometimes getting physical is the only answer, babe. Haven't you found that?"

She shook her head. "I'm not a physical person. I'd rather pump some raucous music and give my emotions free rein."

He shook the water off his hands and glanced over at her. "You've never gone into the gym and hit the punching bag?"

"Well, sometimes I go for a run on the treadmill, music screaming in my ears."

"That works at times, but there are some situations that require a man to step up and settle things the old-fashioned way."

"How is hitting old-fashioned?" she asked. His lip was swelling, and she was a little worried about him. She brushed by him into the intimate quarters of the bathroom and opened the cabinet above the sink. She pulled a freeze pack out of the first-aid kit, snapped it in half, and rubbed it until it was cold.

"Put this on your lip. It'll keep the swelling down."

"Why'd you bring me in here?" he asked.

"Fighting like that in close quarters is dangerous."

"I know. My guys are used to using aggression to break the tension before a mission."

"What tension?" she asked. Men had always been a bit of

a mystery to her. Even her father had been a shadowy figure. She didn't understand how her father could just pat her
on the head when she'd been returned from the kidnappers in
Algiers. But that had been her father's only outward reaction.

"We've been after Andreev for a long time. To know we
came so close to him . . . Well the guys are just jazzed to get
out there and catch him. And losing him at the airport . . ."

"I'm not sure we lost him. I'm tracking two commercial
flights and one charter. We'll find him. We always get our
man."

"Do you?"

There was something in the way he said it that made Anna
blush. "Yes. We are the best at what we do."

"I've heard that about your team, but looking at three
gals and trying to remember they can kick ass is hard."

"What's hard about that?"

"I was raised to protect women."

"Good. Most women do need someone to protect them."

"But not you?"

"No, not me. I learned early on that no matter how much
someone else might want to help you, there's really only
one person you can rely on."

"Yourself," he said.

She nodded.

"Me, too. But you didn't strike me as the cynical kind."

"I'm not. I'm the self-preserving kind."

He gave her a crooked half smile that made him seem very
handsome. She didn't want to think about the fear she'd felt
when he'd been brawling with his men. Not because she'd
feared for him—Jack Savage wasn't the kind of man who
could be hurt physically—no, she'd been afraid because
watching him act like a savage hadn't made him less attractive to her. It had only strengthened what she felt for him.

She needed him.

She didn't know why. Didn't really want to, but there was something about Jack that made chasing Andreev more than just a mission.

For the first time she realized this was what Justine and Charity had experienced. A man had changed their lives.

And she wondered if this mission was her turn. Or was she simply too afraid to be alone? To be the only one of the girls at Liberty Investigations who didn't find something more on a mission?

She'd always been alone . . . and looking into Jack's eyes, she wondered if finally she might find someone who could make her feel safe when she was with him.

Jack was still riding the rush of energy from his fight with Kirk. While it had relieved part of his tension, something new had started to grow as soon as Anna had led him to this secluded room. He'd wanted to be alone with her since the first moment he'd looked into her eyes.

It had changed him, and he wasn't sure he was happy about that change.

"There's something about you," he said under his breath.

"I know. Something annoying, right?"

"Not necessarily."

"Well, there's something about you, too. Something that makes me question things I've always taken for granted."

"What things?" he asked.

"Self-knowledge stuff. Nothing you'd be interested in."

She was wrong. He was interested in everything about Anna Sterling.

There was a loud knock on the door, and Anna gave him a curious half smile before pushing around him to answer it.

"You two okay?" Justine asked

"Fine," Anna said. "How is Kirk?"

"Good. And believe it or not the men actually seem a bit calmer now."

"It's apparently a guy thing," Anna said, glancing back over her shoulder at Jack.

He fought the urge to grab her waist and pull her back into the bedroom. Fought the urge to slam the door shut and lock it and finish what had never really had the chance to get started.

He wanted that woman. And it wasn't just lust for her curvy body. The more time he spent with her, the more he realized he was attracted to every fiber of her.

But she was already seated back at her desk, fingers moving rapidly over her keyboard. He suspected she felt safe there at her desk and in control of the mission as she tracked various flights and coordinated ground transportation for them.

He was impressed by the way she could compartmentalize and focus on the job when just a moment ago he had been concentrating on kissing her. He wanted her mouth under his. Wanted to learn the taste of her so that when she was gone, he'd always be able to recall her flavor.

He shook his head and pushed Anna out of his mind. Despite the fact that Kirk had been out of order with his comments, Jack realized the other man had a point. His men weren't used to working closely with other teams.

Trust had been hard-earned among his guys, and his drooling over a woman on the other team wasn't going to send the right message.

"We good?" he asked Kirk as he took a seat next to the other man.

"Yeah. I think we are."

Hamm cleared his throat. "They want to use the existing trail rail from Algiers into the wilderness area where Andreev's base camp is located."

"What are the options?"

"The train is too public, and after the string of bombings in that area, it is heavily policed now. Getting off when we want to and where we want to will be an issue. I'm working one of my contacts in Algiers to see if we can get two Humvees. It's hard enough to procure one," Hamm said.

"I know. But you're the man for the job."

"That's what she said," Hamm said with a quick grin.

"Indeed," Jack said.

When Hamm left, Jack turned to Kirk. "Once we're on the ground, I want you to use your contacts to set up a buy. Get as close to Andreev as you can."

Kirk nodded. "It's been a few years since I've been in that business, but I'll do my best."

"That's all I ask. We need to play this one close to the chest. I want you in radio contact every six hours."

"Do you want me to stay with him once I find him or take him out?"

"Don't take him out. We need to ask a few questions. Liberty Investigations wants to bring him in alive," Jack said. Sam Liberty had been very clear that they needed Andreev alive to find out how far-reaching his network was.

"Well, that's what Liberty wants. What do we want?"

Jack gave Kirk the savage smile he was famous for. "We want Andreev out of business. But we can't go rogue unless there's no other alternative."

"Roger that. I'll see if I can meet some of my contacts in Morocco. If I disappear . . ."

"I know how to get in touch with you if I need you. Be safe, Kirk. I'm not going to lose another team member to Andreev."

"Don't worry. I'm not ready to get out of the game yet."

* * *

When they landed at a private landing strip just to the west of Algiers, Anna had a moment's pause as she stepped out into the February afternoon. Maybe it was the angle of the sun, but for a moment she was eleven years old again and seeing the White City for the first time. She paused on the stairs of the gangway.

"What's the matter?" Charity asked, pulling her Glock and scanning the area.

"Nothing. Just a bit of déjà vu."

"You have been here before," Charity said. "Are you going to be okay?"

"Yes," she said and walked down to the end of the gangplank. There were two Humvees waiting. There was also a small group of men. Two of them held machine guns and were clearly militia. A third man was dressed in Western garb—a very nice Armani suit, unless she missed her guess.

Charity and Justine closed in on either side of her. The Savage team closed ranks on the women, and Anna was surprised to find herself staring at Jack's back as they approached the Algerian official.

"Welcome to Algiers. I am Yazid Zerhouni with the immigration office," Yazid said in Arabic.

For Anna, Arabic was familiar, but she knew Justine didn't speak the language, so she quietly translated what was being said.

Jack obviously spoke Arabic. He grabbed Yazid's forearm in greeting. "Thank you for welcoming us. Sam Liberty has spoken highly of you."

"And you as well," Yazid said. "Two men from our office will accompany you into the mountains. They are waiting for you inside the main building. Your paperwork is being processed as we speak."

"Thank you, Yazid."

"It is my pleasure. We want the American government to know Algeria isn't a haven for terrorists."

"Our government appreciates that," Jack said.

Yazid led the way to the small buildings at the end of the runway. Anna and the others followed, but she felt the tension in her teammates and in the Savage group. They all knew that no matter what Yazid and his government proclaimed, this part of the world was one where power and firepower went hand in hand. And peace was hard won.

"The women will need to enter through that door. You can meet up in the common area."

Jack turned around to face the three of them. "I'm not sure what we can expect. I know you are all armed, so be careful."

"This isn't our first rodeo," Justine said.

But Anna wasn't offended by his warning. Something about being back in her own personal hell was making it easier for her to accept Jack's traditional male attitude. She knew how quickly the tide could turn here.

"You be safe as well."

The women were separated and then passed through customs. They met Jack's team on the other side, and Anna noticed they were one man short. She wanted to question Jack, but Louis Edmonton was waiting for them. The Interpol agent had been on the same flight as a man matching Andreev's description from Paris.

"Bonjour, *bienvenue* à Algiers. I am Louis Edmonton."

"Bonjour, Louis," Anna said. She noticed that Yazid was talking to Jack. "I'm Anna Sterling, and this is Charity Keone and Justine O'Neill."

One man stood off to the side—a veiled man. . . . She knew the robes were traditional Tuareg garb. She remembered the blue men from her childhood.

"This is Bay Ag Akhamok from the Tuareg. He works

with us occasionally. Andreev's base camp is the terrain of his people. He will serve as your guide."

Anna remembered little of Tamasheq but was able to recall the words of a common greeting. Bay stepped forward and bowed to her. "It's a pleasure to meet you," he said in English.

"Finally someone who speaks my language," Justine said.

Anna had to laugh at her American friend, who was very used to dealing with things on her own terms.

"No offense," Justine said. "I just don't have an ear for languages."

"I suspect you make up for that in other ways," Bay said.

"Yes, I do."

"Where is Andreev's base camp?" Anna asked. She was all for being pleasant, but she wanted to get this mission over with as soon as possible.

"In the southern highlands," Bay said.

"The Ahaggar Mountains?"

"Yes. If you have a map, I will show you," Bay said.

"I do. In fact if you have the GPS coordinates, I can plot it on our map," Anna said.

"I'm going to check on our weapons and on the vehicle we're supposed to be using. I want to make sure everything is ready when you have the coordinates," Justine said.

"Sounds good," Charity said. "Louis, I need the information your agent gathered on the flight from Paris."

Charity and Justine both drifted off, and Anna found a table to set up her laptop. She pulled up the map and started entering the information Bay had for her. He smelled faintly of mint tea, and though he didn't remove his headdress, she could see the faint indigo tint to his skin.

She suspected he was a man of importance to his people. Though the Tuareg were the Blue Men of the Sahara, many of them wore different colors these days. Only a select few kept to the old ways of dying their clothes and skin blue.

"The way we will go is not an easy one," he said after he had given her the coordinates.

"We are used to that."

"Are you? You seem familiar with Algeria."

"I am very familiar with this country. My father once served here as an ambassador."

"Sterling," he said, his voice distant as if searching for a memory.

"Yes."

"You were that girl," he said quietly in Tamasheq.

"What girl?" Jack asked, stepping up next to Bay.

She was surprised that Jack knew the dialect, but she shouldn't have been. He was the kind of man who was very efficient at everything he did. And it bothered her more that Bay might know or remember the girl she'd been.

She shook her head. "That's a story for another time. Bay has given us some good information. Is your team ready to roll?"

Jack looked like he wanted to ask more questions, but she was an expert at keeping her own confidence and wasn't about to push open the gateway to her past any further than she already had.

"We can take a few minutes for your story now," Jack said.

She shook her head. "There are some things I don't ever talk about."

"Maybe you should. It's never a good idea to keep something traumatic bottled up inside," he said.

"What makes you think it's a trauma?" she asked. She didn't want to believe Jack was coming to know her so well.

"You would talk about it if it weren't."

He walked away before she could respond.

Chapter Seven

Kirk left their team in Algiers to try to reconnect with his contacts on Andreev's team. It was difficult to do because Andreev had always played his cards close to his chest and changed his people often. His theory, according to Kirk, was that if you were always reinventing yourself, no one could find you.

And, to be honest, that plan had worked for Andreev for many years. It wasn't lost on Jack that Andreev's downfall had been his attempt at normal life. If Andreev hadn't taken the pseudonym of Ivan and started a family, they would never have gotten as close to him as they had.

It confirmed what Jack's men had been saying on the plane—that women were the downfall of men. That somehow meeting a woman who skewed a man's normal perspective could be his downfall.

Was Anna Sterling going to be his?

"Hell, no," he said under his breath.

"Pardon?" Anna asked. They were in the Humvee, and he was driving, following the coordinates she'd given him. Bay was in the backseat, along with Justine and Hamm. Charity was in the second vehicle with the rest of his team. They had left the beauty of the White City behind and were heading into an area that, during the early nineties, had been dubbed the Triangle of Death.

Being in this business, Jack was intimately familiar with death and with the warring factions of Northern Africa. He looked at the desert landscape and realized the scenery had nothing to do with the brutality of the people. There were some parts of the world where peace was a concept that made no sense. And no matter how hard Algeria tried to bring itself into this new century, there were always going to be people like Bay who clung to the old ways.

"Nothing," Jack said in response to Anna's question. "Are you going to tell me about your past here?"

"No, I am not. But you can tell me about yours. I did a background check on you, Jack Savage, and you don't exist before nineteen ninety-three."

"I don't?"

"Nope. Why is that?"

"Did you spell my name correctly?"

She gave him a look that he was coming to realize meant she was annoyed. "What are you hiding?"

"The same thing as you, I suppose."

"I doubt that very much," she said, a trace of melancholy in her voice.

"We both have something we refuse to talk about. I'm guessing that means we didn't have rosy childhoods."

"Is it only your childhood you're hiding?"

"Not at all. I'm an open book." Jack didn't delve into his past. He'd always believed that each day he survived was another one he had behind him. And that past wasn't anything that needed to be explored and examined. He'd done some things he'd rather never relive. And no matter what traumatic event was in Anna's past, it was nothing compared to the horrors he was hiding.

"Where'd you get that scar?" she asked.

"In Afghanistan."

"What were you doing there?"

"My job."

She reached over and stroked her finger over the one-inch scar on the side of his face. Jack proudly wore the scars of every battle he'd fought in. He was proud of the warrior he was. But when Anna touched him, he felt some of the emotions he liked to pretend he didn't have.

"Your job has taken a toll on you."

"Hasn't yours?" he asked.

She shrugged and looked down at the minicomputer on her lap. "It's different for me. I've been involved in some gunfights or physical fights, but for the most part I spend a lot of my time catching crooks with my computer knowledge."

"You're insulated from the action," he said.

"Yes."

"You live your life that way. Tucked safely away behind your computer while the rest of the world is dirty."

"That makes me sound . . . not very nice."

"I didn't mean it as a criticism," he said. But a part of him did. He was the kind of man who could never stand on the sidelines and let life pass him by. He didn't want to catch Andreev via some sophisticated computer-tracking program. He wanted to be out there in the field. He wanted to cuff Andreev and maybe beat a little justice into his hide. Any man who made his fortune on the blood of others deserved to be brought down in a violent manner.

"Okay," she said.

"What?"

"We're about as different as two people could be. I know that, and you do, too. There's nothing between us."

He glanced over his shoulder, confirming that the occupants of the backseat were occupied.

"We have something between us, Anna Sterling. An attraction even you can't deny."

"I'm not someone who gives in to my baser instincts," she said.

"Yeah, right. We have something else in common."

"What?" she asked. She looked tired, as though she wanted to be anywhere but there. He didn't take it personal, because he sensed there was more to this mission than just catching an arms dealer.

"We both are willing to fight for justice. To make sure the innocent of the world have someone to stand up for them."

"Justice? With a gun?"

"So I'm more aggressive about it than you are. At the end of the day we both want the same thing."

"And that is?"

"For the world to be a better place. A place where children are safe and people can go to sleep without worrying about being shot in their sleep."

She tipped her head to the side. "Maybe there *is* more to you than your warrior body projects."

Demetri hated the mountainous region of the sub-Sahara. There was a reason he'd left this place. And whenever he was drawn back to Algeria, he had that same strangling rage that had first motivated him and Maksim to go into their line of work.

The men around him were leery that he was here; he hadn't been back in three years. He'd seen these men in other parts of the world, but this base camp he had avoided.

It reminded him of the fact that this was his true self. In Seattle, with his wife and children at his side, he could pretend he was a different man. That he'd changed from the boy he'd been.

But here there was no escaping the truth. This crude system of caves was his world now. He was angry, but at the same time he knew this was the way of the world. He was in a part of the world the Americans would have a hard time finding him in.

Unlike the mideast, where there were oil reserves at stake, there was little in Africa for the Americans to come after. And as much as he resented being sent back to this place, he knew he was safe.

He would lie low, continue to broker his arms deals, and take on a new identity. He would have to give up his wife and children, and that bothered him, but he'd lost his family many times, beginning with the small, angry one of his boyhood. Next came the family he and Maksim had created in his early twenties, and now this final family.

How many times did a man have to be burned before he stopped reaching into the fire?

"What do you need from me?" Yan asked.

"Nothing, for now. We will leave in the morning to meet our contacts in St. Petersburg. I want to make sure our stores are secure."

"They are. I will go into Tamanrasset and hire some locals."

That city was built in a *wadi*—a desert valley. And it wasn't a city in the way foreigners thought of a city. To be honest, even *he* wasn't used to the small mountain-village city. He liked the cement jungle and the conveniences that came with it. Most of the men he dealt with preferred that world as well.

"Good. We will leave once you return from hiring them. I want to assemble a new team for this deal with the Sudanese."

"Do you need anything else of me?"

"Not tonight."

Yan left Demetri alone in his room. The sky was brighter
here than in Seattle, and as he stepped outside and stared at
the sky, he wondered what his kids were doing. He couldn't
contact them—had barely had time to tell his wife good-
bye before he'd had to leave the country.

One step ahead of the law.

He'd been on the run his entire life, and he wanted . . .
what? He wasn't the kind of man who could just sit down
and stay in one place.

He had to keep moving.

Demetri opened his laptop, took a glance at the picture
of his kids, minimized the photos, and went to the secure
Web site he used to broker his arms deals.

He had three e-mails waiting for him from men he had
used before. Kirk Mann was one of them. He wasn't sure
how much he trusted Kirk; after all, the man was a mercenary, but, to be fair, no one double-crossed Kirk. He was
very good with weapons, and Demetri had found that his
clients liked seeing their merchandise demonstrated in
competent hands.

Pierre Munro had left a message as well. He was a good
pilot and driver and was excellent in the tensest of situations.

Demetri decided to use both men for the deal in St. Petersburg, but he didn't need them until the end of the month.
He fired off e-mails to both men and then sat back.

This was a far cry from the luxury he liked to surround
himself with, but now that he was here, he was starting to
remember the hungry youth he'd been.

That was one lesson Maksim had forgotten as they'd
aged. You had to be hungry to stay alive. Once contentment
flowed in, so did the mistakes.

And that was exactly what had happened to Demetri in

Seattle. He had gotten a little too comfortable in that silly CFO job with his pretty wife.

He'd started to think he was just like the other men in the corporate world. That was a mistake he wouldn't make again.

He summoned Yan.

"Yes, sir."

"I am going to stay here while you go to St. Petersburg and make arrangements with our client. I want to make sure nothing goes wrong this time."

"Certainly, sir. Is there any reason you aren't leaving?"

"I've been gone too long."

Yan smiled at him. They were cousins on his mother's side, and that branch of the family was loyal to each other— as loyal as men always fighting for money and life could be.

"Yes, you have. It's good to have you back home."

Demetri looked around the cave and silently acknowledged that this was his home. This was the place where he belonged, and if he was going to stay alive and in the game, he would do good to remember that.

"It *is* good to be home. I think it's time we stopped playing games and concentrated on what we're good at."

"Arming the world," Yan said.

They stopped in Ghârdaïa where there were a lot of modern-looking hotels and restaurants. The city was the south of M'zab, which was home to the Mozabites, a puritan culture that didn't really like outsiders. The city of M'zab was picturesque with it's green date palms lining the streets. The drive into the mountains had been long: despite the fact that Yazid had been welcoming, the rest of the people they encountered in Algeria weren't trusting of the foreigners.

They were now on their way into the Sahara, and Anna felt as if she were caught between two worlds. First, the old-world architecture of Algiers's European-inspired city, and now this place, which was near the heartland of Islam.

Anna would rather have kept moving, but the majority of the team knew it would be better to rest now. They weren't that far behind Andreev, and to capture him, they needed to be rested. Well rested. Yet she couldn't sleep.

She had been staring at the ceiling of her room for over an hour now. The sounds outside her window were foreign, and the room itself didn't feel secure to her. She was restless and edgy.

Anna tried to block out those feelings, but the only other subject her mind wandered to was Jack Savage, and she didn't want to think about him. Or about his scarred body and face. Or the intensity in his eyes whenever he looked at her.

She really needed to just focus on the mission, but there was nothing to be done right now. They were all on their way to capture Andreev, and that was it.

Frustrated with herself, she got out of bed and dressed in a pair of black jeans and a long-sleeved T-shirt.

She went downstairs and out into the night, where their vehicles had been left. There was barbed wire everywhere and the kind of security lights that cast no shadow. The world of tourism was foreign in Algeria, but the businesses—like this hotel—that wanted to encourage visitors made it their number-one priority to protect guests.

Anna felt less trapped out here. And she felt safe with her semiautomatic handgun at her side. This was what she needed. Fresh air and exercise.

"Can't sleep?" Jack asked, his voice coming out of the darkness just off the doorway.

"Obviously," she said. She didn't want to see him. He was part of what had her so edgy, and she needed respite from him and the circumstances of this mission.

How had Justine and Charity handled this? The feeling of other things . . . men . . . interfering with a mission? And she knew that they both had been dealing with stuff from their pasts at the same time. Anna felt inadequate as she realized she couldn't cope with it all. She needed the barrier she always used to insulate herself. But there was no computer to hide behind. And Jack Savage wasn't leaving her alone.

Even when they weren't physically together, he was still affecting her. She thought about him when they were apart.

"I'm not much of a sleeper either," Jack said.

"Do you have insomnia?"

"Yes. No doubt because of being such a savage," he said.

"I'm sorry for the comment I made."

"It's okay, I meant it to be self-deprecating."

"Why?"

"Probably the same reason you're wandering around down here instead of sleeping."

She wasn't sure what he meant. "I'm not . . . You want to know what my problem is?"

"What?"

"I'm used to everything falling into place the way I want it to. I like being the one with the most knowledge on a mission."

"Levels the playing field and gives you an advantage?"

"Exactly. But you're something I didn't count on."

"Me?"

"Yes, you. Everything would be so much easier if you really were the savage you call yourself."

"Why would that be easier, Anna?"

"Because then I could ignore you like I usually do men who make me uncomfortable. But you aren't just some dumb macho warrior."

He chuckled. "You say that like it's a bad thing."

"Well, for me it is. I don't like things that don't make sense. There are pieces of you I can't understand that don't fit with what I know."

He walked out of the shadows and over to her. He was wearing a pair of skintight jeans and a dark T-shirt that molded to the contours of his chest.

"You're the same. All precise manners and conservative clothes, yet feisty and kick-ass. You should be leery of holding a weapon in your hand, yet I know that you're comfortable with it."

"That's my training. I'm not hiding anything, Jack. What you see with me is exactly what you get."

He shook his head as he closed the gap between them. He caught her chin in his hand, lifting her face. Their eyes met, and she felt the brush of his breath across her cheek. "That isn't true. You want the world to think you're someone who views the world in black and white, and yet your entire life is based on that gray area in between."

Anna shook her head but knew she was lying to both of them. She hated the fact that she worked in that gray area. That she didn't officially work for any government. But she would never stop doing the job. She believed in what she did, even if she didn't have the sanction from someone in power. "You might have a point."

"I do have one," he said, leaning closer to her. "Slap me if you have to, but I can't go another moment without feeling your lips under mine."

He lowered his head to hers. Rubbed his lips over hers. A slow back-and-forth movement that made Anna stop thinking. She realized this was what had made her so restless.

Not Algeria or the mission. Not the fact that she was unsure of her future.

But this man.

Jack Savage and the unbridled lust he pulled so effortlessly from her.

She felt his tongue against the seam of her lips, and she gave up all pretense of being calm. She reached up to clutch his shoulders and drew him closer to her. She wanted more than his lips on hers. She wanted his hot, hard body pressed against her. She wanted his arms around her.

She wanted him.

She opened her mouth under his, returning his kiss with the kind of passion she'd always wanted to experience but never had.

This man was bringing her to life in a way she hadn't expected. He groaned a deep sound that made her tremble as she tipped her head to the side and gave him greater access to her mouth.

His hands slid down her back, cupping her hips and drawing her against him. He lifted her and carried her back into the motel and up the stairs to his door.

Being alone for an entire evening with a woman wasn't something he usually preferred, but he had the feeling tonight he needed just that. Needed the distance from his team and to spend the night with Anna. Because he had no idea where his personal life was heading. And for the first time since he'd enlisted at eighteen years old, he didn't know what the future held.

Chapter Eight

Jack carried Anna over the threshold into his room. He never slept on a mission—an old habit he'd never been able to shake. Normally he didn't ask for a room, but he was glad he'd taken one this time.

He kicked the door closed, set Anna on her feet, turned and latched the door, and then settled his back against it. She stood there with only the dim light of the moon flickering through the threadbare curtains over the one window in the room.

"No pressure," he said, realizing that with her he didn't want to be as uncouth as he had been with other women.

Sex. Was that what this was? Sex had always been a bodily function to him. But with Anna it seemed it would be more. His itch tonight couldn't be scratched by just anyone—this was a specific craving for her.

"No pressure? Wow, you really have a way with the ladies," she said.

"I know I don't," he said. "But I also know I can't let this chance pass. There is something about you, Anna, that makes me feel . . . Well, it's different."

"Me, too," she admitted in a small voice. "Come over

here and kiss me again. I don't want to think about this too long or too hard."

He pushed away from the door and walked over to her. She looked small and fragile in the wan light and so infinitely beautiful he knew he should just walk away. She was a woman out of his league. But at the same time he'd never been a timid man. And he never backed away from something he wanted. He wanted Anna Sterling.

He leaned down and kissed her. He meant for the embrace to be tender, but with her he had no barriers. So he held her head tightly in his hands and ravaged her mouth. Tasted her as deeply as he could and made her groan in the back of her throat.

She undulated against him, clutching at his shoulders and pressing her body closer to his. He reached for the hem of her T-shirt. Encountering the holster of her weapon was a turn-on for him. This was a woman who, despite the many differences between them, was totally his equal.

He slowly undressed her and then stood back to just look at her. She had none of the scars he had, despite the fact that they worked in the same crazy business.

"Jack?"

"Hmmm . . . ?"

"Are you just going to look at me?"

"Maybe," he said.

But he wanted to touch her and taste her. To make her completely his.

He caressed her shoulder and down her body, tracing the lines of her figure, leaning closer and nibbling on her skin. Her nails dug into his shoulders, and she leaned up, brushing against his chest. Her nipples were hard points, and he pulled away from her mouth, glancing down to see them pushing against his chest.

He caressed her back and spine. Scraped his nails down

the length of it. He followed the line of her back down to the indentation above her backside.

She closed her eyes and held her breath as he fondled her, running his finger over her nipple. It was velvety compared to the satin smoothness of her breast. He brushed his finger back and forth until she bit her lower lip and shifted in his arms. He wanted to give her this dream night—to make it everything for her.

She moaned a sweet sound, and he leaned down to capture it in his mouth. She tipped her head to the side, again immediately allowing him greater access to her mouth. She held his shoulders and moved against him. Rubbed her center over his erection.

God, he hadn't been this hot since . . . never. This was more than just sex, and it was important to him that he make it good for her. He scraped his fingernail over her nipple, and she shivered in his arms. He pushed her back a little so he could see her. Her breasts were bare, nipples distended and begging for his mouth. He lowered his head and suckled.

Jack held her still with a hand on the small of her back. He buried his other hand in her hair and arched her over his arm. Both of her breasts were thrust up at him. He had his arms full of woman, and he knew he wanted Anna more than he'd wanted any other woman.

Her eyes were closed, her hips moving subtly against him, and when he blew on her nipple, he saw gooseflesh spread down her body.

He loved the way Anna reacted to his mouth on her breast. Her nipples were so sensitive he was pretty sure he could bring her to orgasm just from touching her.

The globes of her breasts were full and fleshy, more than a handful. He hardened further as he wondered what his cock would feel like thrust between them.

Jack leaned down and licked the valley between her breasts, imagining his cock sliding back and forth there. He'd swell, and she'd moan his name watching him.

He bit carefully at the lily-white skin of her chest, suckling at her so he'd leave his mark, and when this was over and they were both back to being just operatives on a mission, she'd still have this bit of remembrance from their sexual encounter.

He kept kissing and rubbing, suckling her nipples, trying to quench the thirst, until her hands clenched in his hair and she rocked her hips harder against his length. He lifted his hips, thrusting up against her. God, he wanted to feel her pussy on his cock. Wrapped around him until they were truly one person. He bit carefully on her tender, aroused nipple. She screamed his name, and he hurriedly covered her mouth with his, wanting to feel every bit of her passion for him alone. He didn't want any of his men to hear the sounds Anna made.

Jack rocked her until the storm passed, and she quieted in his arms. He held her close, her bare breasts brushing his chest. He was so hard he thought he'd die if he didn't get inside her.

He glanced down at her and saw she was watching him. The fire in her eyes made his entire body draw tight with anticipation. He carried her to the bed, fumbled for the condoms he carried in his pack, hurriedly stripped off his clothes, and donned the condom before turning back to her.

"You are absolutely gorgeous," she said.

"I'm scarred and battle hardened."

"You're hard," she said teasingly, her hand going to his erection. She caressed him and then moved her hand up his abdomen. Her hands were small and infinitely exciting. He wanted to let her touch him all night, but he was going to come in a second, and he wanted to be inside her when he did.

"Ah, Anna," he said. "You are so tempting."

"Am I?" she asked. He heard the hesitation in her voice.

"You have no idea."

"I'm glad. You tempt me, too."

No woman had ever wanted him the way she did. She wanted him for him despite the man he was. This was more than anything they could explain to themselves or each other.

She reached her hand out to him, beckoning him to join her on the bed. Opening her arms and her legs, she invited him into her body, and he went. He lowered himself over her and rubbed against her. Shifted until he'd caressed every part of her.

She reached between his legs and fondled his sac, cupping him in her hands, and he shuddered. "Stop, Anna. I won't last."

She smiled up at him. "Really?"

He wanted to hug her close at the look of wonder on her face. "Hell, yes."

Jack needed to be inside Anna now. He shifted and lifted her thighs, wrapping her legs around his waist. Her hands fluttered between them, and their eyes met.

He held her hips steady and entered her slowly. Thrust deeply until he was fully seated. Her eyes widened with each inch he gave her. She clutched at his hips as he started moving, holding him to her, her eyes half closed and her head tipped back.

He leaned down and caught one of her nipples in his teeth, scraping very gently. She started to tighten around him, her hips moving faster, demanding more, but he kept the pace slow and steady. Wanted her to come again before he did.

He suckled her nipple and rotated his hips to catch her pleasure point with each thrust, and he felt her hands in his hair clenching as she threw her head back and her climax ripped through her.

He varied his thrusts, finding a rhythm that would draw out the tension at the base of his spine. Something that would make his time in her body, wrapped in her silky limbs, last forever.

He leaned back on his haunches and tipped her hips up to give him deeper access. She scraped her nails down his back, clutched his buttocks, and drew him in. His sac tightened, and his blood roared in his ears as he felt everything in his world center on this one woman.

Jack called her name as he came—and hoped she'd sleep now because if she didn't he was going to curl himself around her and tell her all his secrets. She'd brought him completely out of himself and into a spot he'd never thought he'd be. A place of vulnerability he'd hoped to never find.

Jack didn't "do" contentment, so the fact that he wanted to just lie there with Anna in his arms was disconcerting to him. But her silky curves felt right pressed against the hard angles of his own body. He buried his head in her hair, breathing deeply the sweet, clean-smelling scent.

Anna slept in his arms as no woman had before. He should have been anxious or itching to get away, but instead he felt the rightness of this moment to his soul. He glanced at his watch. They were flying to Hawaii later that afternoon. He wanted to pull her closer into his arms and hold her even more tightly to him so he knew she'd be right by his side forever.

Damn, this was a complication he didn't need. He made himself let go of her and sit up on the edge of the bed.

"Jack?"

"Right here," he said, refusing the impulse to sink back down next to her.

"Is it morning already?" she asked, leaning up to kiss his thigh. He shifted on the bed so he was lying next to her. He shouldn't have been hard again, but he was. Maybe his body realized this night was all the two of them would ever have.

He knew it was only a matter of time before Anna realized she was a princess and he was nothing but the kind of man she should be with. The type of man she should never allow to touch her unmarred body.

"No." He traced a line down the center of her body, lingering at the small mark he'd left between her breasts. He took her mouth in his, letting his hands wander over her, still amazed that she was there with him.

Her stomach growled, and she covered it with her hands. "I can't believe that just happened."

"We haven't had a decent meal since we left DC."

"I know, but I . . . Sorry."

"It's okay," he said, glad to see this proof that she was human and not the sexy angel he'd been imagining her to be. He got up and went to his pack. Rummaging around, he found a protein bar and brought it back to her.

"Thanks."

"You're welcome."

Jack sat back down on the bed and watched Anna eat. She wasn't self-conscious about her body, which was a turn-on. A crumb from the bar landed on the sloping curve of her breast, and she reached to brush it off, but he caught her hand, lowering his head to lick it off. He couldn't get enough of this woman.

She shivered with awareness, and her nipples tightened. He reached for the snack bar and broke off a few more crumbs, letting them fall on her breasts so her nipples were speckled with the food.

He leaned down to lick each nipple until each one tightened further. Then he blew gently on the tips. She raked her nails down his back.

"I'm not really hungry for food anymore," she said.

"Good," he said, taking the remaining part of the bar and scattering bits of crumbs down her body.

Her hand covered his. She leaned up, displacing the crumbs on her breasts. Instead they pooled on her lap and just above her pussy. "How's that?"

"You messed up your breasts," he said, but his hands were already moving lower.

"That's okay. It gives you a reason to fondle me again."

He did just that, taking his time to caress her body before lowering his head to nibble on her stomach. Then he knelt between her thighs and looked down at her.

He rubbed his fingers over her most intimate flesh, dropping the remaining crumbs in his hands on the tawny hair between her legs. She swallowed, her hands shifting on the bed next to her hips.

"Open yourself with your hands for me," he said.

Her legs moved, but she shook her head. Was he being too crude for her? He started to move away, but she caught his shoulders. "Don't go."

"Show me you want me to stay," he said, taking her hands and bringing them to her mound. She hesitated, but then she pulled those lower lips apart. The pink of her flesh looked so delicate, much like the woman herself.

"Hold still," Jack said.

He leaned down, blowing lightly on Anna before tonguing that soft flesh. She lifted her hips toward his mouth.

He drew her flesh into his mouth, sucking carefully. He clutched her hips in his hands, moved his hands up her thighs, pushing her legs farther apart until he could reach her dewy core. He pushed his finger into her body and drew out some of her moisture; he lifted his head and looked up her body.

Her eyes were closed, her head tipped back, and her shoulders arched, throwing her breasts forward with their berry-hard tips, begging for more attention. Her entire body was a creamy delight accented by the moonlight streaming through the window.

He lowered his head again, hungry for more of her. He feasted on her body the way a starving man would, carefully eating out the moist flesh between her legs. He used his teeth, tongue, and fingers to bring her to the brink of climax but held her there, wanting to draw out the moment of completion until she was begging him for it.

Anna's hands left her body, grasping his head as she thrust her hips toward his face. But he pulled back so she didn't get the contact she craved.

"Jack, please."

He scraped his teeth over her clitoris, and she screamed as her orgasm rocked her body. He kept his mouth on her until her body stopped shuddering, and then he slid up her.

"Your turn," Anna said, pushing Jack onto his back.

She took his erection in her hand, and he felt a drop of pre-cum at the head. She leaned down to lick it off. Then she rubbed her hand up and down his penis.

She followed her hand with her tongue, teasing him with quick licks and light touches. She massaged his sac, squeezed his balls, and then made a ring with her thumb and forefinger around the base of his shaft. Her mouth encircled the tip, and she began to suck.

He arched on the bed, thrusting into her before he realized what he was doing. He pulled her from his body, wanting to be inside her when he came.

He dragged her up his body until she straddled his hips. Then, using his grip on her hips, he pulled her down while he pushed his erection into her body.

Jack thrust harder and harder, trying to get deeper. He pulled her legs forward, forcing them farther apart until she settled even closer to him.

He slid deeper still into her. Anna arched her back, reaching up to entwine her arms around his shoulders. He thrust harder and felt every nerve in his body tensing. Reaching between their bodies, he touched her between her legs until he felt her body start to tighten around him.

He came in a rush, continuing to thrust into her until his body was drained. He then collapsed on top of her, laying his head between her breasts.

She smelled so sweet and felt so soft lying in his arms. He'd never held anyone like Anna before, and he knew in that instant he didn't want to let her go. He needed to find a way to keep her, and that seemed like something that would never happen.

Chapter Nine

Anna snuck out of Jack's room while he was in the shower. She didn't recognize the woman who'd spent the last night in his arms. She also couldn't believe she'd actually slept after he'd made love to her.

Algeria was making her crazy.

"Hey, girl, where have you been?" Justine asked as she came down the hall.

Anna blushed, thinking to herself that this was crazy. How was she going to explain this? "I needed some air."

"You have a hickey on your neck," Justine said.

She felt her face turning red. "Leave it alone."

"Okay. I think it's about time you found—"

"It's not like that. I'm not finding anything other than someone to spend the night with."

"Sometimes that's all you need," Justine said.

"Not me," Anna said. She entered her room and headed straight for the bathroom. She should be on her computer tracking information, trolling the black-market message boards so she could find out if Andreev was setting up a new sale. And she suspected the man had to be because he'd want to ensure his business was still on track.

"Do you want to talk?" Justine asked.

Anna paused in her stride across the room, turning to face Justine. "I have no idea what to say. I'm so confused about this."

"Men have a way of doing that," Justine said.

"I know that, but I'm not like you and Charity."

Justine raised her eyebrows at Anna. "What's that supposed to mean?"

"Just that I . . . Oh, hell, I don't know. I think I thought that somehow I was insulated against men, especially men like Jack Savage."

Justine crossed her arms over her chest. "Listen, I know I'm the last person who should be giving advice on men, but it seems to me that Jack is the kind of man you feel safe letting go with because he's not someone you imagine will be in your life for long."

Anna wrapped an arm around her waist. Was that true? Maybe that explained the way she felt this morning because she did feel a certain sense of panic that he wasn't the man she'd thought he'd be.

He'd made love to her tenderly, held her all night, and she'd slept. She rarely slept at home in her posh DC condo, with its high-tech security features. So she had no idea why she was able to sleep solidly in Jack's arms.

"Maybe you're right."

"Maybe? Of course I'm right."

Anna laughed, but inside she was thrown. She knew her life was managed by staying safely behind her computer or weapon—keeping a distance between herself and the world.

Last night had changed all that for her and Jack. He wasn't going to allow her to keep him at arm's length. Or was he?

What if, to him, their night together had been just about shagging? She didn't like to think she'd traded herself so cheaply, but at the end of the day, she'd made the decision to sleep with him.

Did she regret it?

"You okay?" Justine asked.

"Yes, I am. I need a shower. And then I want to check some tracking systems I'm using to see if Andreev is setting up any buys."

"Focusing on the mission isn't always the answer."

"Why not? That's what you do."

"Hey, don't be snippy. I'm just saying that when I was trying to manage Nigel . . . The mission wasn't enough of a distraction. I'm going to see if I can find Charity."

Justine walked toward the door, and Anna felt a moment's thanks that she had a friend like Justine. "Thank you."

Justine turned back to her. "For?"

"Caring."

She shrugged. "Don't let the word out. I have a heartless reputation to protect."

"Your secret's safe with me."

"Good," Justine said. "Did you get a chance to ask Jack where Kirk disappeared to?"

"No. I will as soon as I shower. Is anyone else missing?"

"No. Bay was quiet, and I thought I'd be uncomfortable with him, but he's not like other men."

"In what way?" Anna asked. She'd always had respect for the Tuareg. But, then, when she was kidnapped, the first man she'd seen—besides her captors—had been a Blue Man, and he'd given her a measure of calm before her father had come to claim her.

"I don't know if I can explain it the right way. There's something about the silence in him," Justine said.

Anna smiled. Justine wasn't really an *in touch with her feelings* kind of girl, and a man like Bay—who had the wisdom of the ages and a people not tied to physical things—would be hard for her to reconcile.

"You know I was kidnapped when I was younger?"

"Yes. Why?"

"The Tuareg were the ones to rescue me. They came before the SAS. They came into the cave where I was held. And I was very frightened at first. They were big and dark, veiled from head to toe. But then one of the men knelt beside me and said, 'Be calm, little one.' And you know what?"

"What?"

"It did calm me down. There was that silence in his eyes you mentioned. And I knew no harm would come to me while he was alive."

Justine smiled at her. "Yeah, that's it. I don't like being someplace so far from home and Nigel and Piper. But last night while I was talking with Bay, I felt a sense of ease to that worry."

Anna smiled at her friend. "I'm glad he's working with us."

"Me, too. Though it is odd to have so many men with us."

"I agree. Too many men."

"Or maybe you just don't want Jack with us because he makes you question what you really want."

"As if," Anna said, going into the bathroom. She was very aware that running away wasn't the answer and that her thoughts still dwelt on Jack Savage.

Jack wasn't surprised when he came out from the bathroom into his empty bedroom. He had been surprised that Anna had slept in his arms and that he had enjoyed it. He had liked the feel of her in his arms through the night and had watched her sleep.

Her face had relaxed into something he'd never seen in the short time he'd known her. She was an intense woman who kept her guard up all the time.

But she hadn't last night.

And he felt honored that she'd relaxed herself with him

for those few short hours. He put on his camo pants and black T-shirt just as his cell phone rang.

"Savage."

"Hey, boss. I'm on my way to Andreev's base camp in the Aaggar Mountains. I had to delay a day to make it seem like I wasn't already in country."

"What does he want you to do?" Jack asked. He was already mentally reviewing the landscape. Simply driving into the mountains wasn't going to be good enough. They'd never surprise Andreev, or even find his base, in the maze of the mountains. There were caves and valleys all through the Aaggar Mountains, and sound would carry.

"I'm going to demonstrate some weapons for his clients—same as before."

"Good. Keep me posted when you're in camp. We're working our way to the area—probably have three more days of travel before we get to Tamanrasset. We have a Tuareg guide with us, so once we enter the mountains on foot, we should be able to move quickly."

"Good. Do you just want me to take Andreev out?"

"No. We want to capture him with the weapons."

"I know. I don't know that he stores them in the mountains."

"We'll figure that out."

"Anything else going on?" Kirk asked.

For a minute Jack was tempted to tell his friend about Anna, but he knew he couldn't. His role on the Savage Seven was leader. And showing any hesitation or doubt wasn't acceptable. Besides, Kirk thought women were a distraction the team didn't need.

"Nothing much, just an overnight stay in an area hostile to foreigners. It helps that Anna speaks their language, and Tommy has been doing a good job of passing for an Arab."

Kirk laughed. "Sounds as though you have everything under control."

"Except time. I don't want to let Andreev fall through our fingers again."

"We won't," Kirk said. "If the op seems like it's going south, I'll take him out."

"Affirmative. Make sure you confirm with me before you do."

"I will. When are you guys moving out?"

"We should be hitting the road in an hour or so. I'll have Tommy hang back if you think you'll need backup."

"Nah, I'm good. I've never brought anyone with me before. I think that would spook Andreev."

"Do you need anything?" Jack asked. Kirk worked for him, but in many ways the other man was like a brother. He knew it was clichéd to think of Kirk as his brother in arms, but the two of them had come close to dying too many times for Jack to think of Kirk any other way.

"Nah. Just make sure you stay focused on the mission."

"Kirk, you're pissing me off."

"Good. You pissed off is what we need. You can't lose when you're pissed."

Jack smiled. "Damn straight."

He hung up the phone, grabbed his pack, and walked out the door. His men were gathered in the lower room. Tommy stood when Jack walked into the room. From one glance, Jack could tell the other man was agitated.

"What's up?" Jack asked.

"They don't use the same system we use for wireless communication. I talked to Charity yesterday about it, but I don't think I can get their system to us in time to use when we infiltrate Andreev's camp. We aren't going to be able to get good satellite communication in the mountains. Unless Liberty Investigations has access to some government satellites."

Jack knew snags like this would come up. But they should

have handled this before they'd left the country. "Why is this just now coming up?"

Tommy shrugged. "I think the mission specs changed the equipment they were using. In a city like Paris or even Algiers we could have used two-way cell-phone functions or blue-tooth communicators."

"How are we going to fix it?" he asked, focusing on the radio problems first.

"I'm trying to find a way to temporarily allow our wireless radios to access the same channel the women do. But I need their equipment to make that happen."

"And they won't give it to you?"

"I have no idea. None of the women have come downstairs yet this morning. We're supposed to pull out in less than thirty minutes."

"I'll take care of it. And see if they have access to any satellites. Are you thinking about infrared images of the camp?"

"Yes," Tommy said. "J.P. said a stealth plane probably wouldn't be able to get close enough."

"It won't," J.P. said. "And we need to know numbers of men before we move in. Plus Andreev is going to have some kind of cache of weapons."

"We should be able to get some intel from our man inside. Anyone else got issues?"

J.P. stepped forward. He was the one man on their team who didn't look like a mercenary. His family was old money, and if Jack hadn't stood shoulder to shoulder with J.P. in a firefight, Jack wouldn't have thought the other man was man enough to work in their line of business.

"I think we'll have to go on foot or maybe camel or donkey once we reach Tamanrasset. I don't really have any contacts there. I'd like to go ahead of the rest of the team, but we're short vehicles. I could get a flight, but I don't have papers to fly in this country."

Jack nodded. "Driving, it is. Tommy will wait with me for the women, and the rest of you should head out. J.P., secure transport and set up a base of operations for us outside the main city area. Hamm and Harry, make sure we have the right firepower. I'm not sure we're going to find Andreev's cache of weapons at his hideout, but if we do, I want to have the option of destroying them all."

Hamm stood up, towering over the other guys at almost six feet five inches. "Will do, boss. Should we take the Tuareg with us? He could be helpful with the locals."

"I'll talk to him. Give me a few minutes to talk to the Liberty Investigations team, and then you guys will be good to go."

Jack left his men. He pushed away the softness he'd experienced during the night. He knew what he'd found with Anna was an aberration, not something he should ever get used to, but a part of him mourned that. They were in a dangerous country on an op where one screwup could get his entire team killed. And losing men wasn't something he was prepared to do. He was still haunted by Armand's death.

As much as he liked the man he'd been in the middle of the previous night, he knew he couldn't afford to be that man now.

"I will stay with the women," Bay said, stepping out of the shadows as Jack entered the hallway leading to the stairs.

"Fine. Do you have a contact my men can use to make their jobs easier when they reach Tamanrasset?"

"Yes. Your men should go to my dwelling and garb themselves like me. They will blend in better and get more cooperation from locals. They will need to go to the afternoon market. There they will find everything they need."

"It would be easier for you to go with my guys," Jack said.

Bay shook his head. "I think the women will need both of us with them."

"Why?"

Bay shrugged. "Just a hunch. Something is blowing on the desert wind that doesn't feel right to me."

Bay's words made Jack uneasy, but he'd had his gut reaction come true too many times to doubt the other man.

Anna joined the rest of her team fifteen minutes later. Bay, Charity, and Justine were sitting around a table with Tommy Lazarus. Anna scanned the area for the rest of the Savage Seven but couldn't find them. Maybe Jack had gone ahead with his men. She didn't feel a ping of disappointment at the thought. Really, she didn't.

"I have a lead on two different black-market Web sites. One of them I'm almost positive was Andreev's doing. But it's hard for me to know which of the deals he's setting up," Anna said.

"Good. I think that'll be helpful," Charity said. "You can catch up when Jack comes back. The rest of the Savage Seven are heading to Tamanrasset to get vehicles set up for us to take into the mountains."

"Shouldn't we have someone with them?"

"I need Charity to help get our wireless radios to communicate. Besides, we'll catch up with the men tonight in El Golea."

"I can do the radio thing for you," Anna said. "I have a small computer program I wrote that should help us all communicate a bit better."

Tommy stood up. "Great. Because we don't want to lose the security of the connections we have now."

"We won't," she said. She shrugged out of her backpack and got out her laptop. "Give me a minute to get this up, and I can reprogram all our radios."

"Then I'll ride with the rest of the Savage team," Charity said, pushing to her feet.

"Too late," Jack said, coming into the room. He was mostly in shadow due to the sun streaming in behind him. "The other Humvee is gone."

Anna glanced away quickly, not wanting to look at Jack until she had a moment to get her emotions under control.

"No problem. We won't be that far behind them," Charity said.

Jack was every inch the savage this morning. His jaw was covered with dark stubble, which hid parts of his scars. His blue eyes were dark and cloudy, and Anna felt as though she was seeing the man as he really was.

Was she in any way responsible for this man and for his attitude? Or was she simply channeling her own feelings into his attitude? Last night had probably been nothing out of the ordinary for him. And she had to remember that.

Sam hadn't taken this mission for her to explore her latent issues with men. He'd taken it so they could rid the world of yet another person who thought weapons were the answer to every problem.

"Anna?"

"Yes?"

"Are you ready to go?" Tommy asked.

"Yes. I'm e-mailing you the program. Just reset your radios and we'll be good to go."

She stood up and gathered her stuff, still very aware of the fact that Jack hadn't said a word to her. She felt self-conscious as she finished getting ready and left the common area.

Outside at the Humvee, Anna knew she was in for another long day. She rubbed the back of her neck and then heard the heavy sound of a man's footsteps. She didn't have to turn around to know it was Jack.

He brushed her hands aside and massaged her neck and shoulders.

"I . . . I'm sorry I had to leave this morning."

"It's okay. I expected you to leave sooner."

She turned around so she could see his face, needing to know if he was mad. But he wasn't. Those clear blue eyes of his just stared at her as though . . . as though he was trying to find answers to questions he couldn't define.

"I don't usually do things like that," she said.

He raised one eyebrow at her.

"I know everyone says that to make themselves feel better, but I really don't like to get involved when I'm on an op."

He gave her one of those half smiles of his. "I know exactly what you mean. Screws with your thinking and your reflexes."

"So you don't . . . either?"

She realized she needed some reassurance from him. She needed to believe she meant more to Jack than the sum of last night. But what if that was it? She didn't believe in long-term relationships.

"No, I don't. In fact, that was what Kirk and I fought about yesterday. You are affecting my concentration."

"Is that why he's gone now?" she asked, not wanting to focus on the personal aspect of what he was saying. She didn't want to believe Jack was more than the mercenary she'd pegged him as.

It didn't matter that last night had already shaken her core belief in the things she'd believed. Like the fact that Jack might be more than he appeared. That Jack might be part of the gray area that made her uneasy.

"No, he's working undercover."

"Do you trust him?" she asked.

"Of course I do. Why do you ask?"

"We used a mercenary last fall on a mission, and he got greedy halfway through the op. I don't want to have to pay Kirk more than we already are to get him to do the job he was originally hired to do."

"My men are loyal to me. And Kirk doesn't have the need for more money."

"Everyone says that until they're in a position to manipulate finances to their advantage."

"Everyone?"

"Yes. Everyone. When money is at stake there's no such thing as loyalty or fidelity. You better remember that, Jack."

Anna had learned that lesson when she was girl, and she'd never forgotten it.

"I know who to trust and how far to trust them," Jack said.

"Well, I don't know your team, and I don't share the same faith in them you do," Anna said.

"You do know me, right?"

She shrugged. She did trust Jack, but she wasn't sure she trusted herself or her reactions to him. What if Jack betrayed her the way her father had? Not deliberately, but because of circumstance. She didn't think she could handle that.

"Thanks a lot, Anna. You really know how to make a man feel good about himself."

He pivoted away from her, but she stopped him. "I want to trust you, Jack . . . It's just that I know sometimes life has different plans, and you can be betrayed by someone who would rather die than hurt you."

"I can't change your mind on this, but I do promise you I will never betray you. Even unwittingly."

He walked away, and she let him go, wanting to believe the promise he'd made.

Chapter Ten

Andreev knew Liberty Investigations would be working to find out where he was hiding, but, to be honest, it would be very difficult for them to track down his location. He'd used Algeria for years because the infighting and civil wars in the region made it perfect for his base. Because the government didn't have the time or interest to interfere with his business. And if they did, a bribe usually persuaded them to look the other way.

He wasn't really that concerned with the women finding him. He knew they'd called in backup, which made him smile. Those cocky bitches couldn't come after him on their own. Instead they had gone to a group of mercenaries . . . the Savage Seven.

Andreev had crossed paths with them before, killing one of their numbers, Armand Mitterand. But that bastard had had it coming because he'd betrayed Andreev. Andreev was a very Old Testament kind of man, and this was the place for that. Eye for an eye.

But there was one man on the team Andreev could secretly turn to. He had been careful not to use that connection too often because he didn't like to rely on the past—that weakness had led to Maksim's incarceration. But there were times when he had to.

Yan entered the cavern where Andreev had set up his base of operations. "I have three men from Tamanrasset who will arrive later tonight. I think we should be ready for the demonstration for our buyers in three days," Yan said.

"Good. I have two extra men on their way to help me as well. We need to make sure nothing interferes with this deal, Yan."

"Yes, sir. I will go tomorrow to check the weapons and set up the demonstration site."

Andreev nodded at the other man. "We have a new player after us . . . Liberty Investigations."

"Who are they?"

"A group of independent investigators from the US."

"Should I get in touch with our government contacts in America?"

"Not yet. I have a man undercover working with them. But we need to take extra precautions for this sale."

"I always do," Yan said. "Who is on this team from Liberty Investigations?"

"It's a group of women who work for a man named Sam Liberty. I've been digging around trying to find out more about him."

Yan moved around the desk and sat down. "I can dig around, but my skills aren't really in research."

"I know that. Here are the women who'll be coming after me," Andreev said.

Liberty had a Web site that was very cleaned up and polished.

"We can take on a group of women," Yan said. "Their very sex makes them weaker than us."

Yan was a good man and very old school. While Andreev knew he wasn't going to be captured by anyone, least of all

Liberty Investigations, he'd spent enough time in the world to know women were just as worthy adversaries as men.

"I will make sure the men understand that women may be part of the force that will try to stop the sale," Yan said. "Some men can be blinded by that."

"Indeed they can," Andreev said, thinking of Maksim, who had followed a skirt to his destruction.

"Is there anything else I can do?"

"Not at this time," Andreev said.

Yan left as quietly as he'd come, and Andreev went back to working on figuring out the best way to stop Liberty Investigations. He wasn't concerned with them actually finding his hidden base of operations.

The Aaggar Mountains were vast, and the caves and valleys in the range were hard to navigate. Also there were natural defenses in the area, thanks to the way sound carried over the mountains. No one was going to be sneaking up on him unless they came in on a camel.

And even then he was ready. He wanted to make sure those women paid for all they had taken from him. He clicked his mouse on the photo album and pulled up the picture of his wife and two sons. They were a part of his past, and he knew how hard it was for a young man to grow up without the influence of his father.

He only hoped his eldest, Max, would be as good a brother as Maksim had been to Andreev. Having Maksim in his life had made a huge difference.

And Andreev still mourned the fact that he couldn't see his brother every day the way he'd used to. There wasn't a day that went by he didn't wish he could undo that part of the past. He wouldn't have changed the last ten years or the deals he'd brokered, but he did miss the bond he'd had with his brother.

For all intents and purposes, Maksim was dead to him.

The same way Andreev himself was now dead to his own children. Those boys would grow up without a male influence, and who knew what type of men they'd become.

His only wish for them was that they would be survivors like he was. If he'd taught them anything in the eight short years he'd had with them . . . he hoped it was that.

And speaking of survival, he opened his e-mail and sent an encrypted message to someone from his past. He had lost one life to Liberty Investigations—he wasn't about to lose this life, too. This was the life that was his true self. That life in Seattle had been too soft and too settled. He'd known it wouldn't last and hadn't been surprised when it had ended.

But this life, this place, this was who he was, and he wasn't about to let three women compromise it.

His message was simple and to the point: where is the Liberty Investigations team tonight?

He waited for the response, and when he got it, he smiled to himself.

"Yan!"

A moment later, the other man appeared. "Yes, sir?"

"Do we have any men in El Golea?"

"I'm not sure. I will get someone there. What do we need?"

"I need the Liberty Investigations team stopped there. I don't want them coming any closer to us."

"Very well. I will take care of it."

Anna had never been able to appreciate the beauty of Algeria, and this trip was no different. But the terrain between Ghardaïa and El Golea was making her take notice.

"This is a hard place to eke out a life," Jack said. The two of them were once again in the front of the Humvee. The rest of their group was in the backseat communicating with the outside world to make sure they had the most up-to-date information they could find.

"Yes, it is," she said. "Have you been here before?"

"Not to Algeria, but I've been North Africa before. There is always unrest in this part of the world."

"Why did you choose to become a mercenary?"

He shrugged but didn't take his eyes from the road. The midmorning sun was bright, shining down on them. Jack drove with suberb skill along the narrow highway. "I think it chose me."

"Did it? How?"

"I was with a Special Forces team and got injured. I almost died, as did most of my team. Kirk and I pulled through, and when I got back to the States, I found out who was responsible for that."

When he didn't continue talking, Anna realized that was probably all he was going to say on the matter. She should let it go. Guessing at his age, she could research the matter on her computer and find out what had happened. But she wanted to hear it from him. She wanted to understand this man, who was more than just a comrade in arms. This man who had become her lover last night.

And had changed her perspective on the world without even trying.

She couldn't explain it and didn't even want to try. She only knew she needed to know more about Jack Savage. About the circumstances that had made him into that man.

"Where was that?"

"A bit east of here."

"Afghanistan?"

He shrugged. "I don't want to talk about that time. I was in the Sudan just a little over a year ago."

She didn't ask who he'd been working for or what he'd done there. That was one part of the world that was horrible to even contemplate living or working in. "I've always been thankful I'm able to live somewhere where death isn't an everyday thing."

"I'm not sure I follow that. People die in DC every day."

"True, but not in every neighborhood. There's easy access to a better way of life in the US. Not like Darfur, where your beliefs will get you killed."

Jack pushed his sunglasses up on his forehead and looked over at her. "There aren't many places in the world where you are safe."

"I know that, but we don't live under the oppression of death the way people in this part of the world do. Their governments are so unstable there is never a time of peace."

"That's very true. That's part of what keeps my business going."

"Indeed. So you were telling me how you got started," she said.

"Not now. Why don't you tell me how a Brit ended up working for Sam Liberty?"

To be honest, Anna didn't understand how she had ended up at Liberty Investigations herself. She knew a big part of it was owed directly to Sam. He'd come to find her when she'd uncovered a terror plot involving her supervisor at MI-5. Her supervisor had been reprimanded but not dismissed or brought to trial. Anna had been outraged. There were few things about injustice she could overlook.

"Sam offered me a job when I needed one. He was just forming this team, so he sent me the affidavits on Justine and Charity. I'd been familiar with Charity because she'd been a model in Europe, but I had no idea of her other skills.

"I liked the idea of working on an all-woman team. Sam promised we wouldn't settle for democratic solutions to lawbreakers, and that's something I needed."

"What do you mean, 'democratic solutions'?"

"You know, the kind where someone in power gets a slap on the wrist instead of going to jail."

Jack pulled his sunglasses back down over his eyes. "I'm not a big fan of diplomatic solutions myself."

"I can see that. I bet you're the kind of man who believes in vigilante justice."

"If that's all that's available. I don't like working outside the law, Anna. Don't tell yourself I'm in this simply for the money."

"Then why are you in this?"

"Are you sure you want to know?"

She had the feeling Jack didn't really talk to people that much, and she was flattered he'd take the time to tell her what was going on in his head. He was complicated, this man, and she wanted to uncover all his secrets, peel back all his layers until there were no longer any questions remaining.

She suspected that once she reached his core, he'd be like every other man she'd ever met—and not be as fascinating to her as he was at this moment. But, honestly, she was hopelessly enthralled by him.

"Yes, I do want to know."

"I'm in this business because it's what I'm good at. I was nothing before I joined the army, and getting out wasn't what I'd planned for my life, but I had no choice when I realized that taking orders blindly wasn't for me."

His answer told her they had a lot more in common than she wanted to admit. She supposed they had both left jobs working for their governments for the same reason. And finding this commonality between them made her want to reach over and touch him. To take his hand in hers and let him know he wasn't alone. That in some small way she approved of the man he was.

She didn't say that, of course; instead her BlackBerry pinged, and she answered an IM from Sam.

* * *

Jack didn't like talking period, much less talking about his past, so he had no reason to feel disappointed when they stopped for fuel and Anna got in the backseat.

Bay had climbed into the passenger's seat. His eyes narrowed against the afternoon sun as they pulled into El Golea. His tension communicated itself to Jack, who reached for his weapon, making sure he could get to it in a pinch.

"What do you see?" Jack asked.

"Nothing. It's just that feeling again. Blowing on the wind, whispering to me that there is something. . . ."

"Should we push past El Golea and stop in a less populated town?"

"I don't know. I'm not sure we're going to find accommodations in another area. And nighttime on this highway is dangerous. A lot of guerrillas prey on the unsuspecting folks who traverse this way."

"I think our lodging is at the end of this next street," Charity said, leaning over Jack's shoulder.

Jack drove on through the city. He was alert and ready for just about anything.

When they reached their lodging, no one got out of the vehicle. Anna's fingers were still moving furiously over her keyboard, and Jack knew she was in the process of downloading more information.

"Who found this lodge?" Anna asked.

"J.P. Why?"

"There have been two terrorists incidents here. The last one was only six months ago."

"I trust my men," Jack said, but deep inside he was pissed off. Trusting anyone could be the road to destruction.

"Bay, do you know your way around here?" Anna asked. "I can't get a decent map of this city on my computer."

"I'm not familiar with the city. We should be okay as long

as we stick together," Bay said. "Jack and I will go in and check out the property."

"Do you know something you aren't telling us?" Charity asked Bay.

"No, ma'am. I just have this feeling we're walking into a dangerous situation. That danger may or may not be here in El Golea."

Jack didn't like the feeling that he might have been betrayed by one of his men. To be fair, there weren't that many lodge houses in El Golea that would welcome them. This was the land of the nomadic Berbers, and tourists really weren't welcome in this part of the world. He wondered if they shouldn't just sleep in shifts and keep driving.

But, like Bay had said, there were guerrillas who would not hesitate to attack them. This mission was quickly going through a color change from sugar to shit—something that wasn't helped by him sleeping with Anna last night. Maybe this was his wake-up call.

Jack palmed his handgun as he and Bay left the vehicle and went into the lodging. There was no one at the reception desk, and two old paddle fans stirred the tepid air.

"Where is everyone?" Bay asked.

Jack shrugged. From his experience, when a place like this was empty, trouble lurked around the corner. "Let's get out of here and find another place to sleep tonight."

"Agreed."

They walked out of the building through the lengthening shadows of the late afternoon. But the Humvee was gone.

"Fuck."

He pulled his cell phone out of his pocket just as it vibrated. Tommy's voice said, "You've got company. Get out of the street. We're three klicks from your location."

Jack grabbed Bay's arm and pointed down the street where

Tommy had indicated the rest of the team was located. Just as they stepped back into the shadows, two rough-looking jeeps pulled into the parking lot. The men inside were Berbers, from their dress, and militants, if the semiautomatic weapons in their hands were any indication.

Bay pulled a gun from under his tunic. "This might not be about us," he said.

"Agreed, but we don't need or want the extra attention. We need to get on the other side of the building."

"I'll go first."

Jack nodded and let the other man take the lead. He wasn't familiar with this terrain.

Bay stopped abruptly, and Jack heard the sound of voices. He didn't recognize the dialect but suspected it was an Arabic dialect.

Bay leaned back and spoke in a volume that didn't carry any farther than Jack's ears. "They're looking for the women. They have instructions to make sure they do not leave the city. They believe they have beaten them to this lodge."

Well, that sucked. How had these men found them? He needed to check with Anna to make sure her team was using secure radio transmissions. The men entered the lodge, and Bay and Jack walked past the now deserted alleyway. As soon as they were on the other side of the lodge, they broke out into a jog. Moving quickly down the street, they turned left at the end of the road and saw the Humvee waiting for them.

Jack had never been so happy to see his team. He needed to get them to safety, and then he wanted answers.

He opened the driver's door and saw Anna sitting there. Her face was pale, and she looked pissed off. "Scoot over," he said.

She slid over to the passenger's seat as Bay got in the back. Jack got behind the wheel. A bullet grazed his left arm before he could close the door.

Chapter Eleven

Anna drew her Glock and opened her window to return fire. She heard the sound of Justine returning fire on the other side of the vehicle. Charity was giving directions to Jack, who began driving them very slowly down the narrow street while the men running behind them continued to fire.

Bay was firing as well, and Anna knew later she'd thank God they were all able to function as a team, but at that moment she was just glad Jack was back in the car and unharmed. She'd been so anxious for him when they'd had to move the Humvee.

"Fuck," Jack said.

"What?" Anna asked.

The car sputtered, and though Jack kept his foot on the gas, she heard a whine that signaled the radiator had been hit. "We'll have to dump the Humvee and continue on foot."

"Charity, we need another transport. Take my laptop. I have three areas marked here where we can get something else for transportation." Anna handed the small computer to Charity and then kept her eye and gun on her target. Now that the Humvee was slowing down, their on-foot attackers were closing the gap.

"Damnit. I'm going to floor it around this next corner. We

all need to ditch as soon as I stop the vehicle. Charity, you need to be ready to tell us which direction to go."

"I am."

Jack accelerated, and as soon as they rounded the corner, Anna began gathering her pack and weapons. The Humvee ran out of steam about three kilometers later. They all scrambled out of the vehicle as soon as Jack steered it onto the shoulder of the road.

"We need to head west," Charity said.

They moved in sync, finding the natural cover provided by the barren land and the shadows from the moon.

They fell into an easy formation: Anna and Jack stood guard, while Charity packed up the computer. Bay, Justine, and Tommy were already moving down the street, providing cover for them. As soon as everyone had everything from the vehicle, they were all moving down the street.

"This doesn't feel like a random attack," Anna said as they moved.

"It wasn't. Those men were looking for your group," Jack said.

"How did they know where we were?"

"I guess Sam has a leak, or maybe your radios weren't secure," Jack said.

"Doubtful," Charity said. "We've never had a leak before. Besides, we are it. Sam doesn't have anyone else he'd talk to about this mission except for your team."

Jack didn't say anything, but his face got tighter. "I personally vouch for every one of my guys, Charity. If you call their honor on the table, you're calling mine as well."

"I'm just saying our equipment is better than state of the art, and we never have this kind of problem," Charity said.

Anna knew Charity was really angry. "We had a problem similar to this in Peru," Anna said.

"That was Nigel's person."

"It still affected us," Anna said.

"This is not helping right now," Jack said. "If one of my men is responsible for this, I'll deal with it."

"Is there a chance that could happen?" Anna asked.

Jack just shrugged. She understood he didn't want to admit that one of his guys may have betrayed him.

"I'll do a background check on all your men when we get to a secure location."

"That ought to go over well with Tommy."

"I don't care. And he shouldn't either, if it means we'll all be safe. And you need to know if someone is working both sides," Anna said.

"It wouldn't be for money," Jack said.

"How confident are you of that?" Charity asked. The night shadows were lengthening, which gave them better cover from their pursuers.

"As confident as I can be," Jack said quietly.

Anna reached out and touched his shoulder. "We'll figure this out. However our location was leaked, it won't happen again."

"I agree."

Jack didn't say anything else until they caught up with Bay, Tommy, and Justine. He took the lead in the group, and Anna watched him move. At this moment she saw the truth of who he was. Saw the warrior in him as he managed to get them all through the streets without being seen. When they got to a small compound just outside the city proper, he stopped.

"Is this the right place?"

"Yes," Anna said. "I have an old family friend who lives here."

"Why aren't we staying here?"

"Because I don't like to bring my private life into the missions," Anna said.

Martine DuBreque was an old friend. He was also a missionary she'd met two years after she'd been kidnapped. He'd helped her work through some of the anger she'd felt at not only God but at the government and her father.

They'd kept in touch over the years, but she'd hoped never to set foot in his house again.

She rang the bell and heard the Arabic greeting asking who was there.

"It's Anna Sterling," she said.

Less than a second later, she heard the click of the door lock opening. She opened the door, and they all stepped inside. She tried to appear as if this weren't a big deal, but as soon she saw Martine walking down the cobbled path, still as tall and as big as a bear, she felt very much like the lost little girl she'd once been.

Jack didn't like the scenario this evening. He hadn't been able to get in touch with Kirk. J.P. and the rest of the team had gotten a flat tire halfway between El Golea and In Salah, and now he was in the house of a man who insisted on putting his hand on Anna's shoulder every time he spoke to her.

Jack knew a big part of his anger stemmed from two things. One was that someone on his team may have been responsible for leaking their location, and two was that Anna could have been injured or killed.

Those men who had come after them weren't the type to just let their victims walk away. Even though he'd seen the evidence with his own eyes that Anna could take care of herself, he was still edgy. He really needed five minutes alone with her so he could kiss the hell out of her and reassure himself they were both alive.

Tommy was seated in a formal sitting area that looked

like it was used by some sheikh from an old-time movie. "I want you to stay on the radio until you find Kirk. Then let me know you have him."

"Yes, sir. Do you think it was someone on our team who leaked the location?" Tommy asked.

They all remembered the night Armand had died, and it had been a lot like this—things going wrong, communications failing . . . "It better the hell not be."

"That's what I'm thinking. We have to be able to trust each other."

"Damn straight. Don't say anything to the other guys about what happened."

"Yes, sir. I . . . I mentioned to J.P. that we're getting another vehicle."

"That's fine. Does he have any contacts here?"

"None. I trust J.P. the way you trust Kirk."

"Well, you weren't the one who was set up. The women were. Do you know anything about that?"

"No, sir," Tommy said, stretching his long frame on the ridiculously over-cushioned couch. "Do you think Andreev sent them?"

"Yes. He's not going to take a chance on getting captured. And he'd know about the women from the embezzlement investigation."

Tommy stood up. "I can't stand this room."

Jack laughed. "It seems like something out of a movie set."

"You got that right. I also don't like sitting still. Feels like we're waiting for them to find us."

Jack felt the same way. But this wasn't just a Savage Seven op. Regardless, they were going to get the hell out of there as soon as humanly possible. The less time they spent around Martine the missionary, the better Jack would feel.

"While you're monitoring the radio I'm going out to his

garage to find us a vehicle. I want to be on the road before the hour is out."

"Do you think the girls will go for that?" Tommy asked.

"Not if you call us girls," Justine said from the doorway.

"Damn, I always get called out with my mouth," Tommy said with a smile that even the hard-nosed Justine positively responded to.

Jack envied Tommy his easy way around women. He glanced over at Justine. "Is Anna ready to go?"

"Not yet. I couldn't take another minute in that room. It's too dark and weird."

Jack definitely liked Justine. She was simple and straightforward, as uncomplicated as Anna was complex. "It *is* dark. I'm going to secure transport."

"I'll come with you. Charity's in there talking about Eastern philosophy. Sometimes I really feel like the dumb one who likes to blow things up."

Jack laughed at that. "There's a lot to be said for blowing things up."

"True that."

They left the main house and walked through a flowered pathway to the garages. "Have you met this guy before?"

Justine shook her head. "Nah, but Anna knows people all over the world. Sam probably would have hired her just for her contacts."

"Why did Sam hire her?"

"She's a freakin' computer whiz. She can get any information on her machine. And she's pure magic as a sniper. You should see her work. I'm more of an in-your-face fighter, but she's the best there is at a distance."

That sounded like the woman he'd come to know. She liked to fight crime, but from a distance, so she didn't dirty her hands.

"Why did Sam hire you?"

"Because no one else would," Justine said. "I don't want to talk about it."

"No problem," he said. "I'm the same way about my past."

"That's good to know. You're a good shot. I was impressed with your driving."

"Thanks," he said. "I was trained by the best."

"I could tell. You remind me a bit of a guy I used to know."

"Who?"

"My dad," Justine said.

"Thank you," he said quietly.

Justine grabbed his arm. "If you hurt Anna, it won't matter who you remind me of. I'll come after you, and you'll find out what it's like to be up and close and personal with a very pissed-off American woman."

Jack shook his head. "I'm not interested in hurting anyone."

"Good. Then we won't have any problems."

Anna let Charity and Martine's conversation flow around her. She was dealing with too many memories. She should have stayed out of country instead of coming with the team. Algeria wasn't a place where she could handle the past and the present.

And that wild ride through the streets of El Golea had been more than she'd needed today. Jack had kept them safe, and he'd driven with the skill she expected of him, but she didn't like it when things didn't go according to plan.

"Will you excuse me, Martine? I need to check a few things on the computer before we can leave."

"Certainly, Anna. If you need anything at all that I can provide, please let me know."

"I will. Thanks for the use of your garage and the shelter here."

"It is my pleasure."

Anna left Charity with Martine and went to find a quiet space. The only room unoccupied was Martine's silly harem room with the big pillows and colorful fabrics. She grabbed her backpack and pulled out her laptop. She used her scrambler to make a secure connection to the Internet and started going through the pasts of the men on the Savage Seven team.

She plugged in all their names and waited for the files to come back. She didn't want to suspect Jack's team, but she knew men, and she had been betrayed too many times in the past to ever really trust anyone.

Perhaps a big part of her attitude had been formed in childhood. It was odd, but she'd never been able to really feel safe, even with her father at her side. But then the Blue Men of the Tuareg had made her feel safe.

She couldn't explain it.

She heard footsteps and glanced up as Jack walked under the archway. She was very happy to see him, which was silly—a feminine reaction to the fact that he had walked into a dangerous situation.

He crossed to her side and took the laptop from her, setting it carefully on the floor before taking her by her shoulders and drawing her to her feet.

He wrapped his arms around her, and she couldn't help but cling to him. To hold him as tightly as she could. She tilted her head to the side, and their eyes met a second before their lips met as well. She closed her eyes, overwhelmed by the emotions she felt.

She tunneled her fingers through his close-cropped hair. He smelled familiar, and his warmth wrapped around her, warming that part deep inside her that was still shivering. She wasn't afraid for herself, she realized, but for him.

She had been in more dangerous situations, and she had always survived.

Jack lifted his head from hers but kept his hands on either side of her head. "I was so damned worried about you."

She shook her head, reaching up to touch the scar on the side of his face. "Don't be. You're one hell of a driver."

"I'd rather we didn't have to put ourselves through that again."

"Me, too," she said. "I was looking through the files of your men. Can you help me make sure I've got the right guys?"

He rubbed the back of his neck. "If it's one of my men . . ."

She hoped it wasn't one of his guys, but frankly, with the team as big as it was, it had to be someone on the inside. And Anna knew it wasn't Charity or Justine—not because of blind loyalty, but because she'd known the women for so long.

"Well, Kirk is undercover with Andreev's men. You should find a connection between the two of them. He's worked for Andreev in the past to demonstrate the weapons for potential buyers."

"Thanks for that. Why didn't you talk to us about this before you sent him out?"

"There wasn't time."

She shook her head. "I don't think that's it at all. I think you didn't trust us."

"Perhaps," he said. "The point is moot because now you know."

"Maybe we can use him to set up Andreev."

"I'm sure we can. I'll let you speak to him the next time we talk."

"Not me," Anna said. "Charity is the logistics person."

"Then Charity. The next person you should look up is Tommy Lazarus."

Anna typed Tommy's name, and she heard Jack curse as the information started scrolling down the screen. She had access to Interpol and other law-enforcement agencies around the world, so there was little information she couldn't access.

"His military record is supposed to be sealed," Jack said.

"Dishonorable discharge . . . Did you know about that?"

"Yes. He had his reasons for what he did."

"But that shows a flagrant lack of respect for authority," Anna said.

"No, it doesn't. It shows he has the sense to think under a tense situation and not just blindly follow orders. That's the kind of man I want at my back."

Anna realized this was more than a difference of opinion—they were philosophically on opposite sides of this issue. She had been upset with her supervisor for being a criminal, and she had turned him in, but she wouldn't have gone into the office and kicked his butt.

Jack shrugged. "Most of my guys have something like this in their past."

"Do you?"

"What do you think?"

"I think yes, you do. You aren't the kind of man to blindly take orders."

"You've got that right. I'm also not the kind of guy who can walk away from something like betrayal. If one of my guys leaked our location, they'll pay for it."

Anna wasn't sure she liked the sound of that, but she kept working, pulling up background information on Jack's team. At first glance there didn't seem to be anything obvious about the men, but she kept digging. Somewhere there had to be a connection to Andreev, and she was going to find it.

Chapter Twelve

Jack didn't like the fact that Anna was easily finding information on his team's background, but he knew his own past was well hidden and that his secrets would stay buried.

His connections at the Pentagon owed him too much to ever allow found a connection to the man he used to be. Jack Savage, mercenary, was all the world ever needed to know. The man he'd been had been a necessary evil in another time and place. And his death and subsequent rebirth as Jack Savage had been well hidden from the world.

"This is interesting," Anna said, pointing to her computer screen. He couldn't help but notice that when she leaned forward, her breasts were outlined by the khaki-colored T-shirt she wore.

"What did you find?"

"Well, it might be nothing, but Harry Donovan isn't an American. Did you know that?"

"Are you sure? He was in the military. I guess he could have been a permanent resident of the US."

"Let me check on it. I think he was born in Europe and raised in the former Soviet Union."

"What the fuck? I think I would have heard about this before now."

"Why?"

"Because we work for the CIA."

"Hold up . . . let me check one more thing." Anna kept her fingers moving over the keyboard.

Jack stood back and watched. All thoughts of seduction were pushed to the back of his mind. If Harry had been lying to him for all this time . . . He didn't let himself complete the thought. There was nothing to do right now except find the leak, if there was one, and stop it.

"Well, he became a citizen in nineteen ninety-seven. But he was raised in what is now Serbia in a boys' home. That's the connection I was following. I think Demetri and Maksim Andreev were raised in the same facility. Now, I don't know how old Demetri is, but their paths could have crossed."

"I can't accuse one of my guys on a hunch, Anna. I need hard facts."

"Okay, I can respect that. Give me a few more hours, and I will know for sure. Until then I think we should keep all information between us."

"Agreed."

Anna looked perfectly at home in this movie-set room. Jack knew they didn't really have any time, but he wished he had time to make love to her on these cushions. In this lush room, Anna tempted as no one else ever had.

But he would probably screw up seducing her. He knew he had been too crude and probably too blunt last night. Even though she hadn't minded at the time, he had had the feeling that in the harsh light of day he would come up lacking.

"Why are you looking at me like that?" she asked.

He shrugged. "How am I looking at you?"

"Like you want to do more than kiss me," she said.

"Maybe I do."

She tipped her head to the side. "Jack—"

"You guys ready to roll?"

Justine looked like an ad for *Soldier of Fortune* magazine. She'd changed into dark desert camo pants and a khaki T-shirt and had a bandolier of bullets around her chest.

"Yes," Anna said. She hit a few keys on her laptop and stood up. "We're done here, for now. Is everyone else ready?"

"Well, Tommy and Charity are out in the truck talking to Kirk. I think we're going to try to set up the buy with Andreev's customer."

"Good. We should get out there and see if there's anything Anna can add to their plans," Jack said.

He didn't want to think how close he'd come to dropping his guard once again with Anna. He would have kissed her in another second if Justine hadn't come in. And that would have left them both in a very awkward position. He wasn't the kind of man who made those types of amateur mistakes.

He walked away from the women as they were talking. He knew it was rude, but he had to get his head around two things—that Harry might be selling them out, and that Harry wasn't the thing that was really bothering him.

No, what really made Jack uneasy was the fact that he hadn't wanted to leave Anna. That he wanted to spend as much time as he could by her side. Damn the consequences. And that was how men like him lost their edge.

Maybe he was already slipping, and that was why he'd missed the thing with Harry.

They drove most of the night. The Land Rover wasn't as big as the Humvee, but there was plenty of room for everyone. Anna had taken the front seat again next to Jack. She was coming to like sitting next to him. She had her computer running, searching for information and connections on Jack's team and on their own. In the backseat, everyone was quiet.

Anna wasn't sure that someone on Interpol hadn't leaked the fact that they were in Algeria and on the path to intercept Andreev. And as much as she wanted to believe that the information had been accidentally leaked, she couldn't. She knew human beings were fallible.

She watched Jack's face, illuminated in the lights of the dashboard, and regretted the fact that they wouldn't be able to spend this night in each other's arms. And not just because she still craved his body with an intense lust she wasn't entirely comfortable with, but because she wanted to feel his arms around her. She wanted to take some comfort from that big male body of his.

"You're staring at me," he said, his voice pitched low.

"Yes, I am."

"Don't."

"Why not?"

"Because you make me think about stuff that has nothing to do with our mission."

Good, she thought, but didn't dare say it out loud. "Are you always a single-focus guy?"

"Yes, without exception."

She'd love to have his single-minded attention on her and only her. But she knew she wasn't the kind of woman who wanted a man like that. That had never mattered to her before. But with Jack—she did want that. "Sorry."

She turned back to her computer, reminding herself that she liked her life from the safety of her computer. She didn't get close to anyone, because when she did, that left her room to be let down.

Even Justine and Charity had let her down. No one had ever *not* let her down. She didn't want to have any disappointment from Jack, so that meant it was better to leave things alone between them.

"It was nice of Martine to lend us this vehicle."

"Yes, it was," Jack said. "How do you know him?"

"My father was an ambassador for a number of years. And we always met interesting people. Martine was one of them. He's a missionary."

"I know," Jack said. "He told us before I had to leave."

"That's right, you did hear a little talk. He's an interesting man."

"Interesting is one word for it."

"What word would you use?"

Jack shrugged his big shoulders. "I don't know. He's not my kind of guy."

"Why not?"

"He talks too much."

"I can see how you wouldn't be able to relate to a guy like that. I mean, you're more of an action guy."

Jack glanced over at her. "Yes, I am. Is that a problem?"

"No. I think your ability to take charge saved our lives this afternoon. I know we could have outfired those guys, but your quick thinking and driving made a huge difference."

"Thanks."

"You're welcome," Anna said. "You're not what I expected."

"I'm not?"

"No. And I know that comment makes me seem a little ditzy, but I just expected you to be all mercenary. And you're not."

Jack passed a bus on the highway and then again glanced over at her. "In what way?"

She felt silly starting this conversation, but she wasn't going to back down now. "You really care about your guys."

"That's no big thing. We aren't a group of mercenaries brought together for one mission, we're a team. We function like a family."

She had a thought and didn't censor it. "Do you have any family?"

He shook his head. "Not for a long time. But the men on my team are like brothers to me. Some of them do stupid things, but I know when the chips are down that they have my back."

"It's that way with me and Justine and Charity. I always felt a bit of the odd man out until I was teamed with them, and then I realized exactly what I was meant to do. I fit with them. If that makes any sense."

Jack reached over and squeezed her thigh. "That makes perfect sense to me. It's the same with my team. Well, a little different because I'm the leader and your team seems to be more a group of peers."

"Yes, we are. I think we all have issues with authority, but your guys need to know the pecking order. Probably because you all came from the military."

"I agree. Chain of command is important to us. I think that's why I didn't consult you guys before I sent Kirk out. I'm used to being the final decision maker."

"I can see that you are. When was the last time you took orders?"

"I take them every mission when we sign up for a job. There are always ROEs for each op."

"Rules of engagement. You even talk like you're still in the military."

"It's the only language that makes sense to me. I know you don't like the gray areas in life and that you think mercenaries are a necessary evil, but we aren't really gray."

Anna saw that. She understood now that men like Jack

and his team did a job a government couldn't do. Like this job to apprehend Andreev. All governments wanted Andreev arrested and out of business, but no one would have authority to enter Algeria and track him down—only someone who owed their alliance to no government.

Jack pulled into the secure location—where the rest of his team was waiting in In Salah—at about three in the morning. Everyone in the Land Rover was alert and ready to move. They had guns drawn and were tense as they got out of the vehicle.

They was only one hotel in the city, and they made their way through the lobby. The desk clerk was visibly taken aback when they entered, but he helped them, and soon they were all upstairs in their own rooms.

Jack wandered around his room, wondering what kind of information Anna was going to find on Harry. A part of him wanted to go to the other man's room and confront him tonight. Find out if the son of bitch really had sold them out.

But instead he was standing here in the moonlight wishing like hell he'd had an excuse to bring Anna to his room. He had never needed anything, but now he needed her.

No, that couldn't be right. He didn't need anyone. He didn't even need his team. Not really. It was nice to have them because of the consistency they offered on the job, but he didn't need them.

Hell, who was he kidding? He was almost forty and had crammed more living into those years than most people. He wasn't going to sleep, and he wanted to be with Anna. He gave up pretending he didn't and went down the hall to her room.

Jack picked the lock on Anna's hotel room door using the

key card he'd swiped from the front desk. He eased into the room. There was a glow from the computer in the corner, but otherwise the room was completely dark.

He kept his eye on the lump in the bed. Anna hadn't moved since he'd entered the room. He knew he shouldn't be there, but he'd needed to be with her, and somehow coming to find Anna had seemed the saner of his two options.

He felt the air stir behind him. Anna grabbed him around the throat with her left arm and took hold of his right wrist with her right hand. The barrel of her gun was wedged against his ribs. "What are you doing here, Jack?"

The cool cotton of her shirt rubbed against his back. "I thought we could talk."

"And you couldn't knock on my door?"

What was he going to say? The truth was that he hadn't wanted her to turn him away. Wasn't sure he would have left if she'd said she needed to be alone tonight.

"No, I couldn't knock on your door," he said, bringing up his left hand to grasp her left wrist, covering her moving fingers with his own.

She caressed his neck with her fingers, rubbing his pulse point.

He held her hand firmly in his grip and shifted his weight. He liked touching her too much to let go. "Do you really want to wrestle like this?"

"Not really," she said.

He eased her down on the bed and placed his body on top of her. "Unless you want me to go," he said.

"No. Stay with me, Jack," she said, wrapping her arms around his shoulders as her legs shifted so he was nestled between them.

This was what he'd been wanting since they'd arrived in

El Golea. He'd needed to touch her like this. He knew he had no right to her, no claim on her, but he'd needed it.

He bent and kissed her. She bit at his lower lip, sucking it between her teeth. He groaned deep in his throat, palming her breasts through the T-shirt. Her nipples responded immediately to his touch.

She gasped, and he thrust his tongue into her mouth. He captured her wrists and held them to the bed by her head. He undulated against her, using his entire body to stroke hers.

"Link your fingers together and put them behind your neck."

"Why?" she asked, rubbing her toes up the back of his leg. She was so sexy with him, it was almost like she was someone he didn't know. He wanted her like he'd wanted no other woman.

"Because I said so," he said, pushing his hand up under her T-shirt and feeling her smooth skin. He put both hands on her waist and lowered his head to her chest, listening to the steady beat of her heart.

"Jack?"

She ran her hands down his back, holding him close to her. He shuddered at her touch and knew the the cause was more than physical. "I thought I said hands behind your neck."

He felt the minute shifting of her body beneath his and was ready when she pushed her heels against the bed and rolled them both over. When he was underneath her, he pulled the T-shirt and underwear from her body and tossed it aside. He cupped her breasts with both hands, rubbing his thumbs over her nipples.

She undressed him, slipped on a condom, and then shifted on top of him, straddling him. He felt the humid wetness at the apex of her thighs, and he hardened painfully. He shifted his hips, rubbing his length along the center of her body.

Anna moaned his name, scraping her fingernails down his chest. Jack slid his hands down her torso until he had her hips in his hands. He teased her with the tip of his erection, rubbing it at the gate of her body. Her hips rolled against his, and he groaned at the feel of her, so hot against him.

He felt a drop of pre-cum bead at the head of his erection and knew he wasn't going to last much longer. He thrust up into her at the same time he rolled them so that she was once again underneath him.

Fully seated inside her body, he held himself still, even though he wanted to thrust until he came. He angled his head and caught the tip of her left breast between his teeth. He bit carefully on it and then suckled her deep into his mouth.

She shifted under him, trying to move herself on his cock, but he held her underneath completely under his will.

"Jack . . ."

Sweat beaded along his back as she tightened her inner muscles around him. Damn, maybe he wasn't in charge after all. He slowly pulled back so that only his tip remained inside her. He shifted his mouth to her other breast before thrusting deep inside her again.

He grabbed her hips and held her still when she would have met his thrust. She tightened herself around him again, but this time he was ready for it.

"Lift your legs, Anna. Bend them back to your body so I can get all the way inside you."

She did as he asked, and he slid all the way home. He buried his face against her neck, inhaling deeply the scent of this woman, and began to thrust slowly in and out of her body. He wanted to claim her as his own, but he knew he couldn't, knew that he and Anna only had this brief time in

Algeria before they had to part ways and go back to their normal lives.

She gripped his ass, running her fingers lower until she scraped his sac with her fingernail. The feel of her touching him made him boil.

He increased his thrusting until he felt her start to again tighten around his body. Anna threw back her head and screamed his name. He quickly covered her mouth with his and thrust deeper into her until his own orgasm rushed through him.

Breathing heavy, unable to move and unwilling to separate himself from her, Jack rested his head against her breast, licking at the sweat on her skin. Her hands stroked up and down his back. He wanted to lie here forever and forget there was a dangerous world outside the door.

Chapter Thirteen

Anna woke up in Jack's arms after the second-best night of sleep she'd gotten in a long time. The warmth of his naked body pressed to hers dispelled the lingering coolness of the night.

She rested her head on his pectoral muscle and felt his hand on her hip. He was stroking her torso. There was some latent sexuality to the movement, but she sensed that he was simply touching her without the intent to arouse her.

Too bad that wasn't working. She tipped her head back and looked up at him with sleepy eyes.

"Good morning," she said.

He leaned down and kissed her, rubbing his lips on hers and pulling her more fully into contact with him.

"Morning," he said as he lifted his head.

"Did you sleep at all?" she asked. He didn't look tired, but she could tell he hadn't rested. There was a battle-hardened look in his eyes that told its own story.

"No. But I usually don't."

She hugged him closer to her. "I'm sorry."

He squeezed her. "Why? Because you got some sleep? You needed it. It doesn't take a rested brain to fire a gun, but it does take one to work the computer. And you're a whiz at that."

"Thanks," she said. "I really should get up and check on today's route. I asked Sam to check on activity in the region so we know what to expect."

"Good. I'm going to talk to my men this morning. I'm not taking any more chances on our safety."

She nodded. If there was one thing she was coming to understand about Jack, it was that the job and this team were his life.

Suspecting Harry of being in league with Andreev was not an easy thing for Jack to think about. He stroked his finger over Anna's face, down the curve of her jaw, and then to her neck.

"You are so pretty for someone lethal."

Anna knew men found her attractive, but she'd never really been comfortable with labels. Inside she was always a mass of contradictions, and none of her self-image was driven by how she looked. "Thanks."

"Don't say it like that. I meant it as a compliment."

"I know. You haven't really seen me lethal yet."

"I saw you shooting yesterday in the Humvee. You have a precision I've seen only in snipers."

She shrugged and reached up to touch his stubbled jaw. "I'm not like you, who can do two things at once. I really can concentrate on only one thing at a time."

"That's all you have to do."

She rested one elbow lightly on his chest and looked down into his face. "I'm glad you came to me last night. I really wanted to see you."

"Why didn't you walk down to my room?"

She shrugged her shoulders, unsure how to put her insecurities into words. Maybe it was the fact that they had seen Martine just that afternoon, and he reminded her of her uncomfortable past and distrust of men. Or maybe it was the fact that as they'd driven through the dark and dangerous night, she'd tried to put into perspective the danger Jack had been in, and she was scared at how terrified she'd been of losing him. Or maybe it was the fact that she was starting to really care for Jack Savage. A man she knew very little about. She really knew only what he'd told her. And that petrified her.

She struggled to find words, and that's when she realized she was changing. She knew the process had started months ago when Liberty had taken the bodyguard case with Daniel and she'd watched Charity fall in love. Then the process had continued when Justine had fallen for Nigel.

There was something about Anna that had irrevocably been altered by those events, and there was no going back.

But that didn't mean she wanted to talk about it with Jack.

She rolled to her side and sat up on the edge of the bed. She wasn't sure she liked this new direction of her life. Was she really falling for Jack? Or was her emotional attachment to him simply a reaction to her friends' attachments to their men?

She rubbed the back of her neck as she sat there, lost in thought. Jack put his hand on the small of her back. Though it was just his hand, she felt the warmth of him spread throughout her entire body.

She glanced back at him and saw something in his eyes that reflected the turmoil inside her. Her computer pinged, telling her she had a new message, and she used that as an excuse to turn away from Jack.

She got up, finding her T-shirt on the floor, and pulled it on. She walked over to her laptop and tried to ignore the sounds of Jack as he moved around behind her.

She checked the message from Sam, who said he had a

contact near Andreev's camp in the Aaggar mountains. And that his contact had been approached to take out the women of Liberty Investigations.

She e-mailed Sam back, thanking him for the intel, and then got out her BlackBerry and IMed both Charity and Justine. They all needed to be on their guard, now that they were targets. This wasn't the first time a client had gotten squirrelly on them, but it was the first time they'd had someone of Andreev's stature after them.

Andreev was a man at home with weapons and death. A man without conscience who had spent his entire adult life peddling death. And now he was gunning for Anna and her friends, and she aimed to do everything in her power to keep him from succeeding.

"You okay?" Jack asked.

She hadn't realized he was standing, reading over her shoulder. "Yes. This just makes me more determined to catch Andreev and put him away."

"I won't let anything happen to you," Jack said. "That's a promise."

Jack still didn't like the thought of Harry or anyone else compromising the safety of the group, so after he and Anna were both showered, he met with her, Charity, and Justine.

"The only way we're going to expose the leak is to set up a dummy site for your team to go to. I've looked at the maps, and I think we should say we've decided to stop driving to Tamanrasset and instead put you three on a flight to the city."

Anna nodded. "I like the idea of this trap, but to be honest, we can't put a planeful of civilians at risk."

"I agree," Jack said. "Do you have the contacts here to get a charter plane?"

Charity pulled out her BlackBerry and hit a few keys. "I might be able to get us one. Let me go and make a call."

"Don't go too far," Jack said. "As soon as my team sees you're all alive and well, a call could be placed to Andreev."

Charity nodded.

"Why don't we just put your men in a room, and then I'll go in there with my guns and we'll have a talk? I guarantee someone will talk," Justine said.

"Maybe because we aren't the Sopranos," Anna said. "Again, I like this plan. It gives the man who leaked our location a last chance to redeem himself."

Jack doubted redemption was going to be in the cards, but he hoped like hell it was. The Savage Seven were his family, and he didn't take lightly to the fact that one of his own would betray him. "I'm more of a mind to follow Justine's suggestion—"

"Right on," Justine said. "There's nothing wrong with a little old-fashioned American persuasion."

Anna shook her head. "If Charity can't get a plane, I'll radio Martine and ask him to send one. But if this plan works out, I have the feeling we're going to see a plane blown up."

"That's exactly what I think will happen. It should reveal our leak and give us an edge if Andreev thinks he's killed the three of you," Jack said.

"Why isn't Andreev trying to kill you as well?" Anna asked.

"I suspect he thinks he can buy me," Jack said.

"That's the crux of the problem with men who sell their sword to the highest bidder: there's always a higher offer."

"You have to learn to goddamn trust me, Sterling. I haven't betrayed you yet."

Anna flushed and looked away.

Jack knew his words were angry, and he didn't give a damn. He was pissed off at everyone this morning. And hearing Anna say the same thing she'd said so many times before about men bothered the hell out of him. He wasn't going to sell out her or Liberty Investigations—no matter how much money he was offered.

He stalked to the window, his mind already going over how he could protect the women. Logically he knew they could take care of themselves, but he couldn't go against his baser instincts. Yesterday had been harrowing because he hadn't entertained the possibility that they'd be in danger until they'd reached Tamanrasset. He'd thought the journey would give them the time they needed to gather information and get ready to capture Andreev.

He heard Anna's step behind him a minute before she put her hand on his shoulder. He glanced down at her small hand on his shoulder, and he felt a surge of testosterone. He was a big man, a strong man, and no one would harm this woman. His woman.

He took a step to the left, out of the view of the window.

"I'm sorry about what I said. I know you wouldn't sell us out for money," she said.

He stared down at her. "What *would* I sell you out for?"

She tipped her head to the side, watching him with those serious blue eyes of hers. "I think you'd sell us out if we did something that betrayed your honor. Something that made you question our integrity. But otherwise you aren't going to budge from our side."

He knew better than to let himself feel any kind of warmth toward Anna—it was bad enough that the lust had turned into the kind of desire he knew he was never going to quench. But her words made him feel good. Made him realize there was a part of her that got the fact that he was the kind of man who lived by his own black-and-white rules. "Thank you."

She smiled up at him. "You're welcome. Now come back

to the table and let's finish figuring out how to plug this leak Andreev is manipulating."

He followed her back to the table. Justine said nothing as he sat down, but she'd been poring over a computer map of the local airport.

"Is it possible Andreev has some kind of leverage on Harry?" Anna asked. "I hate to keep fixating on him as the leak, but he's the only one with a connection."

Jack had no idea. "Harry's not the type to form attachments. He lost his brother in Operation Desert Storm. I don't think he has any other family."

Anna carried over her own laptop. Her fingers moved quickly over the keyboard as she studied whatever information she'd accessed. Jack stayed where he was, looking for a good place to set up an ambush.

"If we use this hangar, we should be able to set a trap for Andreev's men."

"I agree. I have a few RPG launchers, but they can be a bit dangerous, so I think we should stick with semiautomatic rifles and handguns," Justine said.

"I agree. We don't want to piss off anyone else in this area. The Berbers have been hospitable, for the most part, and we still have to go into the mountains to capture Andreev."

There was a knock on the door. Jack went to it and asked, "Who's there?"

"Bay."

He opened the door and let the veiled man enter. Bay stopped in the doorway. "Your team knows we're here and that there was an attack on the women."

"Who told them?" Jack asked.

Bay shook his head. "I'm not sure anyone did."

* * *

Anna didn't like the tension in the bedroom as all five of the Savage Seven guys (Kirk was still with Andreev), Bay, and the Liberty Investigations team sat there discussing yesterday's attack. She carefully watched all the men on Jack's team, trying to see if any of them revealed in their expression anything that could be a lead. But they didn't.

"Now that we can communicate easily, I think we should stick together," Tommy said. "We can definitely take on whatever Andreev sends if we operate like a team."

"I agree," J.P. said. "I think the Liberty team should be considered part of our group for the duration of this mission. Anyone who attacks them attacks us."

Anna smiled at J.P. J.P. and Tommy were both very old-fashioned in their views toward women, and they were outraged that Andreev had dared try to kill them.

"I don't know. I think if the women are safely in Tamanrasset with Bay, we can concentrate on going into the mountains and finding Andreev's base," Hamm said. "It's not that I don't want you ladies around, but if Andreev is concentrating on finding you, we can sneak up on his flank."

Anna agreed that it made a certain kind of sense. But she also knew a team divided fell more easily. She used her laptop to make a note to keep investigating Hamm. Was there something she'd overlooked about him?

"I don't like it. I think we should stick to our original plan," Harry said. "Just keep moving on to Tamanrasset in the vehicles. We know he wants to stop the Liberty team from getting close, so we can watch out for his next attack."

"Well, as we are essentially your boss for the mission, *we* will be deciding what our next move is," Justine said.

She saw Harry bristle. Anna wondered if something as simple as not liking to work with women would have been enough for any of Jack's team to sell them out.

"Where's Kirk?" Harry asked. "He should be here if we're dealing with an aggressive threat from Andreev."

"He's working another angle on the mission. He'll join up with us tomorrow in Tamanrasset. For now, I appreciate everyone's opinion, but as Justine said, we are working for the Liberty team, and we will bow to their wishes on this."

Charity stood up and moved through the throng of men. "We have discussed this with Sam, and it is of paramount importance that we don't let Andreev scare us off. Getting to Tamanrasset is the next step for us to apprehend him."

"We should go as a team," J.P. said again.

"I think the best thing is for us to go ahead. We will use Bay and the Liberty Investigations resources to get everything in place," Charity said.

"Okay, then, that's what we'll do. We need to start arranging for a plane and securing a hangar at the airport," Jack said.

"I'm on it," J.P. said. "Do you know if there's a private hangar or landing strip we can use?"

"There is," Anna said. She walked over to J.P. "Bay went over there this morning and secured it for us. We will use this one."

J.P. leaned over her shoulder to look at the computer screen. "I can send it to Hamm, and he can distribute it to you all."

"Please do," Hamm said.

She sent it to J.P. and then thought about the rest of the team. Jack thought they should just set the trap and see who walked into it. But Anna wanted to keep all the men covered so they could catch the culprit in the act.

"J.P., Harry, and Tommy should go with Hamm to the airport. You can take the lead vehicle. We need to secure the route," Jack said.

"I'll take Justine, and we can walk the route first," Bay said.

"Won't that be dangerous?" Harry asked. "I mean, women stand out here."

"She will be Tuareg when she leaves this room," Bay said.

Anna didn't smile, but the thought of her petite friend dressed as one of the veiled men of the Sahara was a bit funny. She had the feeling they'd draw a few stares, but she knew Justine was good at pulling anything off. And they had already worked out a cover story for Bay to use if they drew too much attention

"Fine," Jack said. "Charity and Anna will stay with me. I will personally make sure they are safely brought to the hangar. I want a call from J.P. when you guys have the area secure."

"I'm on it, boss. Yesterday wouldn't have happened if I'd been there," J.P. said.

Anna felt a little better hearing J.P. She didn't like the thought that someone on Jack's team had sold them out. It made her think that maybe they all just wanted Liberty Investigations out of the way so they could proceed with taking down Andreev however they wanted.

She didn't know what Jack's mission objectives were outside of theirs. If he had been given the chance to go after Andreev on his own, would he have simply killed the weapons dealer and said the hell with the government officials who wanted more information from him?

"I guess that's it for now. Everyone get their gear together and we'll head out in twenty minutes," Jack said.

Anna noticed the hard look he gave each of his men as they walked out of the room.

Chapter Fourteen

The airport hangar wasn't exactly modern, but Jack had seen worse and didn't let that affect him.

He hated the fact that he was setting up his men, but he had no choice. He couldn't put the rest of his team in jeopardy. And he needed to know whom he could trust.

He'd been betrayed once—that had been the action that had set him on his present course. This present life where he was Jack Savage and no longer the man he used to be.

"You ready for this?" Anna asked.

"Yes, I am. Are you?"

"Of course," Anna said. "Men trying to kill me makes me angry."

Jack laughed.

"My kidnapper was an attaché at the British Embassy. He was working for another government as well as ours."

Jack sobered immediately, surprised that she'd revealed that part of her past, but it made everything click into place. "No wonder you like to have as much information as you can on everyone."

"Yeah, it's my Achilles' heel. I have to know everything, otherwise I can't relax. On this job . . . well, I had you flagged as a potential problem."

"Me? Why?"

"Because you didn't exist until ten years ago. And if you think I can't tell that someone has been all over your file making up stuff, you are sadly mistaken."

He arched one eyebrow at her. "I'm not about to deny it. The men who changed my identity did so for a very good reason, angel."

She blushed. "Tell me why they're hiding the truth of who you are."

"They're hiding it because I wasn't the kind of man a government likes to admit is one of theirs."

She suspected it would be something like that. "What did you do?"

He shook his head. "Not now. The past has no relation to the man I am today. And we have to move out."

"I'm not going to stop digging," she said.

He stopped abruptly, bringing them chest to chest. "You aren't going to find anything that will make you sleep easier, angel. Leave it be."

"I can't," she said. "I know you want me to, but until I know everything . . . You could just tell me."

"I can't. I never speak of it," he said, turning back toward the front of the hangar. "Where's Charity?"

"Charity?" Anna said into her wireless mic. "Are you in position?"

"Affirmative. Are you?"

"I am. Savage is going to be moving into position in a moment. Justine?"

"We're almost to the airport. The Savage team is moving quickly down the street in formation, protecting the vehicle Charity is driving."

The plan was simple. Charity was driving the Land Rover that was supposed to have all of them in it. Jack and Anna were in sniper positions around the hangar they would be using. All Jack's men had been left alone so that whoever was feeding Andreev information would be able to contact him.

"Now we wait," Justine said.

"And pray." Bay's voice came over the radio. "Perhaps this exercise will be for naught."

"What does your instinct tell you?" Jack asked. He'd moved away from Anna, so she heard his voice just like everyone else—in her ear.

"That all this work isn't in vain," Bay said.

"We will soon see," Charity said. "Justine, let us know once you're in position in the hangar."

"I will. We haven't had enough time to set up surveillance. Do you know the hangar is secure?" Justine asked.

"Negative," Anna answered.

"Hold up. I'll secure the location before you enter," Jack said. He was on their frequency and also monitoring his men on another radio. "I'm going to switch over to my men and warn them that you'll be slowing down, Charity."

"Affirmative."

They all heard Jack click on the second radio. Anna knew he'd been careful to keep it muted while he was talking to the Liberty team and Bay.

"Savage here. We are in a holding pattern until I can ascertain the security of the hangar."

"Affirmative, boss. Do you need backup?"

"I never have before," Jack said.

"Let us know when we can continue on in. Charity?"

"I'm listening," Charity said. "The team and I are waiting for Jack's go."

"Good," J.P. said.

Anna lowered herself to the ground, her sniper rifle set up on the grassy terrain. She had wanted to go with Jack. But she was a better shot from this distance, and she was needed to provide a lookout for the entire area.

She scanned the airport runway and noticed nothing new. There were still the two trucks that had been parked at the terminal and the one private plane that ferried passengers to Tamanrasset.

"You're clear to the hangar," Anna said.

"Affirmative," Jack responded.

"I don't have a heat-sensitive scope on this rifle, Jack, so I can't see inside the building. The schematics I looked at earlier show two doors, one to the west and one to the south. If you enter through the south, I can provide the best coverage."

"Affirmative," Jack said. Anna saw him making his way in a quick, low jog across the open area leading to the hangar. Then he opened the door and disappeared inside.

Anna cursed under her breath as she realized Savage shouldn't have been Jack's name. It should have been Maverick because he was such a damned loner. She strained to see in the darkened hangar, holding her breath, and then heard the report of shots coming from the building.

"Coming in behind you," Justine said.

"Good, Jack is in trouble."

"We'll all move together," Bay said.

He and Justine were by Anna's side in a minute. Bay bent and cut the fence around the airport. Anna picked up her sniper gun and folded the stand. She needed to get closer and make sure Jack was okay.

Bay peeled the fence open, and Anna stepped through first. Justine and Bay followed. In a crouching run, they made their way across the open field. The sound of gunfire continued as they ran across the tarmac.

"Charity, the airport is not secure. Keep an eye on the Savage Seven, and we will report in once we have the hangar secure," Anna said.

"Affirmative. Do you need me?"

"Not now. We can handle this. We do need you to keep all of Savage's men under surveillance."

"Will do."

"Savage, we're coming in through the south door. Is there anything we need to know?" Anna asked.

"Three gunmen. Two wounded, one dead. The two are heavily armed. I'm pinned behind the Piper Cub plane."

"We'll bring firepower and help you out."

"Anna, stay low. They were ready for me when I walked through the door."

"Will do. Are you injured?"

"I'm fine. Just get in here so we can take back this hangar."

"Affirmative."

Bay led the way to the hangar, handgun drawn, eyes alert behind that heavy indigo veil. He reminded Anna so much of her past that for a moment all she saw was the night she had been rescued.

"Anna?"

"I'm fine," she said to Justine, realizing she had fallen behind. "Let me get into position before you two enter. I'll provide ground cover."

"Good idea," Justine said.

"Tell me when you're going to enter," Jack said.

"We're in position now," Anna said. She sent cover fire into the building and then stepped back to let Bay enter. She heard his gun as he fired a couple times. Then Andreev's men fired on them. Justine cursed and went in with a low, rolling dive.

Anna stayed in her position, firing carefully into the hangar. Now they had the other team outnumbered. She continued providing cover from her location.

She had just prepared to enter the hangar when a bullet sped past her, brushing her long hair and grazing her face. She felt the burn from the bullet but knew it hadn't cut her skin. *That was a little too close for comfort,* she thought. She flattened herself on the ground and reached for the machine gun she had slung over her back.

Jack, Justine, and Bay were already firing. She glanced at the plane: there was no way they would have made it to the aircraft, and even if they had, someone had cut the fuel line—she saw a burgeoning puddle under the plane.

Bullets continued to be exchanged around her. Anna looked at Jack and Bay to see if either of them were going to come over. But they were busy, and Anna made her decision. She needed to end this firefight now.

She stood in the doorway and opened fire, which drew out the two remaining gunmen.

Bay, Justine, and Jack all continued firing in the direction of the assailant, covering each other. Whoever was firing was making judicious use of their bullets. Anna figured the person must be a trained sniper because only the fact that Justine, Bay, Anna, and Jack weren't presenting clear targets seemed to keep them from being shot.

"Damnit, Anna," Jack said. But she knew he was taking advantage of her bravado.

"Only one bastard left," Justine said.

"Not for long," Bay said.

A minute later they had routed all the gunmen in the hangar. Two lay prone and dead; a third one was wounded but still conscious.

"Now it's time to get some answers," Jack said.

"Can I bring the guys in?" Charity asked.

Jack looked like a savage as he stared at the man on the floor. "Yes, I think you better."

"Do you recognize this man?" Justine asked.

"Yes. He's done some work for me before."

Anna felt the pain Jack must have been experiencing.

She was in pain from the bullet burn on her face, and her arms ached from holding the sniper rifle and machine gun. But she didn't relax her guard. Neither did Bay. He had gone to the door to the west and taken a position as guard.

"I'll cover the south," Justine said. "Give me the machine gun."

Anna passed the machine gun to her friend and turned back to Jack. He had the man by his collar. "I want to know who hired you, Edward."

The other man just smiled at Jack, and Anna knew in an instant this was going to get dirty and ugly. There was no other way for this to end.

Jack hauled back his fist and hit Edward square in the jaw. Edward's head snapped back, and blood dribbled from his lip. "Demetri Andreev. And he has plenty of men like me to keep sending. He wants the women dead, Savage. And he's not going to stop until they're taken completely out of the game."

"Then he doesn't know me very well, because I have enough firepower to make sure whomever he sends goes back in a body bag."

"You got lucky this time, Savage. Next time he will send more men."

"You won't be around to see it," Jack said, hitting Edward again, this time knocking the man out completely.

"We've got company," Justine said just as seven men roared into the hangar on the back of a military-style jeep. They burst through the large hangar door in a fire of bullets.

"Shit."

Anna hated the fact that this fight wasn't going to be a quick one. They hadn't gotten any answers from Edward, and now they were dealing with more armed men. She dropped her sniper rifle and pulled out her handgun, firing at the men as the jeep came to a stop.

Jack shot the driver directly between the eyes. Justine let out a rebel yell and dove for her opponent. The men climbed out of the jeep, moving in a rough formation toward them.

Anna dropped back into the shadows, waiting for the right moment to make her move. She kicked her opponent as he moved past her position, knocking his weapon from his hand. He countered with a one-two jab toward her face. The blow connected with her cheekbone, stunning her. She pivoted into the punch and spun around to attack again, this time connecting with her opponent's ribs.

He moaned and stumbled backward. Anna's breath ripped in and out. Damn, her face ached from the punch and the bullet burn. She analyzed her position and realized she had to put her body on autopilot. She ceased thinking about everything but surviving. This guy was twice her size and smelled like he hadn't bathed in about a week. She wouldn't be able to call herself much of an agent if she couldn't bring him down.

Anna diverted a blow to her head—she hated getting hit in the head. She spun away, but he grabbed the back of her hair, pulling her up short. Anna brought both of her hands together and reached behind her head for his wrist, applying a firm locking technique. She twisted her body, ducking under his arm. He tried to kick her, and she lifted her leg and kneed him in the groin. He moaned as she twisted his arm behind his back and forced him to his knees.

She stooped beside him and brought his hands together, using a zip cord to cuff him. She patted him down and found two guns and a knife. She took the weapons and put them in her pack.

Winning always brought its own kind of high. Anna had

forgotten how good it felt until this moment. She didn't examine it too closely but tucked the information away for later.

She left that guy bound and headed toward Jack a few feet away. He was holding his own with two assailants. She was impressed with his hand-to-hand skills. He had to be one of the most skilled martial artists she'd ever met. While she used a mix of tae kwon do and the street fighting her dad had taught her in hand-to-hand combat, Jack seemed to be using an ancient art form with deadly skill.

But he still was just one man. Justine and Bay were occupied, so Anna took a deep breath and a minute to analyze the fight. She jumped into the fray at Jack's back, feeling truly alive in the moment, fighting back to back with Jack. Each of them was equal in this moment. There were no secrets between them, and they functioned well together.

She'd been bred for this, and she realized—as she fought with an energy that seemed to come from deep inside—that this was what she'd been missing when she'd hid behind her computer and waited for information to come to her. She liked the physicality of this moment. She disliked the fact that she'd denied this part of herself for too long.

"Let's finish this," she said to Jack.

"I'm trying," he said, connecting solidly with his opponent's sternum. Then he used a judo chop to the neck.

The other guy attacked Anna with a strong kick that knocked her into Jack. He grunted and steadied her. "You okay?"

"Fine," she said.

She was aware of Jack fighting behind her, but she focused all her energy on *her* fight. This guy had pulled his knife and now took a swipe at her leg. She kicked the weapon from his hand and out of reach. Knowing she had to make this attack count, she concentrated on hitting his neck and head. She hit him hard in the chest with a front kick, forcing his head to connect with the wall. Jabbing his neck with her elbow, she grabbed one of his meaty wrists and brought it up behind his back. Forcing his hands together, she cuffed him.

She turned to help Jack, but his opponent had fallen to the ground in a crumpled heap. Jack cuffed him.

"The Savage team will be at the hangar in less than five minutes," Charity said to them over the mic.

Justine and Bay had their guys bound, and they maneuvered all the men into a small group.

Jack pulled his handgun and kept the assault rifle loosely at his side. "I want some answers."

"You're about to get them," Charity said.

"We are armed to the teeth," Anna said. "I'd hang back if I were you, Charity."

"I'll provide outside cover," Charity said.

"Me, too," Bay said.

"Justine and I will stay here with you," Anna said to Jack.

"I can handle this on my own."

"That's what I'm afraid of. We need answers, not dead bodies."

Jack looked over at her. He rubbed his hand softly over the bullet burn and bruise she could feel forming under her left eye. "Dead bodies work for me. We need only one man to talk."

"But we aren't uncivilized. And you've already sent a message to Andreev by breaking the men he sent to attack us."

"You could have been hurt, angel. Seriously hurt."

"I'm okay," she said. "I knew the mission specs before I agreed to come here."

"Yes, you did. But you didn't expect to be betrayed by someone on your own team. You and Justine can stay, but I will handle this my own way."

Chapter Fifteen

Jack was angry. Well beyond angry. Sending this much manpower after the Liberty Investigations team meant Andreev didn't want them off his tail—he wanted them dead. And knowing that one of Jack's people had set them up like that . . . set up Anna like that . . . made him want to kill.

He tried to remember he was no longer a killing machine, but some things were too deeply engrained into a man. And for him, it was killing.

His men walked into the hangar in total radio silence, and they looked ready for action.

"What the hell happened here?" J.P. asked. "Is everyone okay?"

"The good guys are," Justine said.

"Anna's bleeding," Hamm said. "I've got my medic kit with me."

Hamm moved forward, but Jack put himself between his men and the women. "Not yet. Someone sold us out. There was no way for Andreev to know about this except from one of you."

No one said anything. Jack watched his men and knew he wasn't going to find an answer the easy way. "Fine, we'll do this the hard way. *One by one.* Harry, come with me."

"Why me?" Harry asked. He shifted his AK-47 into a more maneuverable position in his arms.

"We need to talk to everyone," Anna said. "The rest of you can wait here with Justine and Bay."

"I don't like this. Why do you suspect one of us, Jack?" Hamm said. "And that wound on Anna's face should be disinfected and covered."

"I suspect one of you because we controlled the information. As you all know. So one of you had to be the leak."

"Why not the women?" Harry asked.

"They were with me the entire time."

"So it's automatically one of us," Harry said.

"It would have to be," J.P. said. He moved away from the other guys so no one was at his back and he had a better vantage point.

All the men began to do the same. Their unit had been honed in fire. They didn't trust easily, and Jack could honestly he say he understood the men and why they were the that way. But this moment hurt. He had tried to build the Savage Seven into a unit—a family—and now one of them had torn that family apart.

"I don't think you should do it one on one. We all need to know who's responsible," Tommy said. "Whoever betrayed us put Jack and I in the line of fire yesterday."

"I agree," J.P. said. "So which one of you bastards is working both sides on this one?"

No one said anything, and Jack knew they *were* going to have to do this the hard way.

"Anna, tell them what you found."

"Um . . . I found out that Harry isn't an American by birth and that he grew up in the same group home Demetri and Maksim Andreev grew up in."

Everyone turned to Harry.

"So? That doesn't prove anything!" Harry said.

"No, it doesn't," Anna said. "What do you have to say for yourself, Harry?"

He nodded his head. "I . . . I did give him some information on your location."

The team converged around Harry, and Jack moved toward his men. "I want to question him."

But fists were flying, along with accusations. "Did you sell out Armand, too?"

"I hope you spent the money you made because you aren't going to be able to enjoy it now," J.P. said as he hit Harry in the jaw.

"Stop it!" Anna said.

"He has it coming," Justine said.

"We need more information from him. We don't need him barely able to stand up."

"My men deserve a chance to deal with this," Jack said. "This is an internal issue."

"No, it's not," Anna said. "We need to know how much has been compromised."

Jack nodded. "Back off, guys. Let's give Harry a chance to speak."

Harry spit out a mouthful of blood, but Jack noticed he didn't say anything about the beating his men had given him. "I never sold out Armand. This was different."

"Explain that," Jack said.

"The women aren't part of our brotherhood, and Jack is different with them around. He's compromising our team."

Jack noticed his men didn't jump to his defense. "I thought we'd settled this on the plane."

"No, we didn't. All we accomplished was that Kirk disappeared, and you're working with Liberty Investigations more closely. Your loyalty should be to us," Harry said.

"I don't condone what Harry has done, but you're a different man on this op, Jack," Tommy said.

"Jack has to be a different man. Your team hasn't been able to apprehend Andreev in all these years. No organization has done it," Anna said, and as much as Jack appreciated her coming to his defense, he knew that it wasn't really helping.

"Armand died so we could capture Andreev." Jack said. "And, Harry, no matter what you tell yourself, you are directly responsible for this fuck-up. And there is no way we are going to let you get away with saying my attitude is to blame."

"Fine. What are you going to do with me? I don't work for Andreev. And I want to stay with the team."

Jack looked at his men. "That's not up to me to decide. You betrayed everyone when you decided to give up our location."

"When will you know?" Harry asked, wiping blood from his nose.

"I'll keep an eye on Harry," Bay said. "The rest of you go talk this over. But we need to make a decision soon and then move out."

Anna didn't like the way Jack had stood aside and let his men beat the crap out of Harry. Sure, she didn't like being betrayed, but beating a man like that . . . Surely no leader would think that was acceptable.

And when she and Jack had fought back to back, she'd felt they had enough in common to make up for the fundamental differences between them. But what had just happened made her doubt that.

"Here," Hamm said, handing her an antiseptic wipe and a Band-Aid.

She reached up to clean the burn on her face, but Jack

took the wipe from her and drew her away from the others. "Talk among yourselves," he said to them.

He walked Anna to a corner of the hangar where they could be alone. His hands were gentle as he tended to her wounds. And when he leaned down and kissed her cheek, she wanted to melt. Hell, she did melt a little inside, despite the fact that she was still horrified by the way he'd let his men beat Harry.

"What's the matter?" he asked.

"I can't believe the brutal way you dealt with Harry."

Jack shrugged. "It's the way we are. We have to be able to believe the man next to us has our back. And Harry betrayed that. I'm surprised it wasn't worse than it was."

He was touching her so tenderly she was having a hard time reconciling both sides of the man he was. "You really are a savage."

"Have I ever tried to convince you otherwise?"

"Yes," she said. "When you held me so carefully in your arms."

"That's different. That's . . . I can't explain it. But it has nothing to do with the type of man I am as a leader."

Anna stepped away from him. "You can't be so different."

"I am. And don't act like you haven't done the same thing. How did you treat the mercenary who kept upping his price on you in Peru?"

"I didn't beat him bloody," Anna said. But she knew she'd wanted to. If she'd been able to get her hands on the man who'd been their only hope for keeping Piper safe until Justine and Nigel got to Piper, Anna would have done something vicious.

"He tried to kill you, angel," Jack said, drawing her closer and wrapping his arms around her. "I know my men think

I'm too rattled by you to do my job, but I'm not. If anything, having you on this team makes it more important to me to make sure we're all safe."

"Why?"

He shrugged. "I don't know. I mean, I know we have nothing in common and outside of this place in time we make no sense, but, Anna Sterling, I am not prepared to let anyone harm you. And if someone does, they should be prepared for the consequences."

Anna felt oddly touched by his words. She knew they didn't make sense in the real world, and she had no idea what life would be like when they got back to DC.

She realized she wanted to enjoy every moment she had with Jack. She couldn't sanction the beating he'd allowed for Harry, but she did understand what had motivated it.

"Jack, there's something about you that makes me very glad to be a woman."

He smiled down at her. "I'm thinking of you as *my* woman."

She wasn't sure she liked that. She belonged to herself and had always been comfortable with that. But Jack was changing the way she looked at the world, and maybe belonging to him was something she could handle.

He leaned down and kissed her. The embrace was tender and sweet. He traced the seam between her lips with his tongue and then slipped inside.

She wrapped her arms around him and rose on tiptoe so their mouths were fused together. She brushed her tongue over his. He breathed her name, and she held him tightly to her, burying her face against his chest. She felt his chin come down on the top of her head, and for a minute she just stood there, absorbing his strength.

She liked the feel of Jack's hand against her face. He made her feel cherished and beautiful—two things she could safely say she'd never experienced before. But that didn't mean she knew how to handle it or him. That she even wanted to.

And she wished she could give a little of this peace in her soul to him because she knew he had a gaping wound inside at being betrayed by one of his men.

And that was something no one should have to experience. Brothers at arms should always be able to count on one another. It gave Anna another perspective into the reality of Jack's world. She wondered if he was savage because that was the way the world had made him.

"Why are you looking at me like that?"

"Because I just realized I don't really know you at all. And that might not be a bad thing."

"You know me better than you realize," he said. "Let's get this business with Harry settled so we can get on our way to Tamanrasset. I don't think I'll have a moment's peace until we've captured Andreev."

Anna didn't say anything, but Jack had shaken the part of her she'd always taken for granted, and she knew she was going to have to figure out how to be herself again.

And she wasn't sure how to do that.

Jack and Anna rejoined the rest of the team. Jack didn't like the way everyone looked at them. "What's the decision on Harry?"

"We've discussed it, and J.P. will stay with Harry every second until he proves himself to us. But we don't want to lose him," Hamm said.

"We all don't like working with women," J.P. said. "No offense, ladies. But you're throwing off our normal rhythm, and that may have contributed to Harry's actions."

"I'm not ready to forget what he did," Tommy said, "but

as long as one of stays with him twenty-four–seven, I think we'll be okay. If he does anything like this again, he's out for good. And we put the word out so other mercenaries know he can't be trusted."

"That sounds fair to me," Jack said. "I'll give Harry the news, and then we need to head out. This took up too much time. Every day we delay in getting to Tamanrasset is a day closer to letting Andreev slip through our fingers."

"While you do that, we'll get the vehicles ready to roll," J.P. said.

"And I'll get the local authorities to take care of this bunch of riffraff," Justine said.

"We can't allow any of them to go back to Andreev and talk," Jack said. "We need to find an alternative for the men."

"I'll see what I can do," Charity said.

Jack walked away without looking back. He knew Anna wasn't going to approve of his actions. He didn't expect her to or need her to. He had to remember for the sake of his men and the team he'd built that he was in charge. There wasn't going to be any more discussion about what they did. He'd survived in this world a long time by carving his own path.

And Anna Sterling wasn't going to derail him now.

To the left of the plane, Bay and Harry stood quietly talking together. Bay had no weapon trained on the other man, and Jack respected the man though he couldn't understand his behavior. But, then, to Bay, Jack imagined they all seemed pretty strange.

"Thanks for watching him. You can go back to the group now."

"I will," Bay said, bowing to Jack before walking away.

"The team voted, and you can stay on with a babysitter. If you screw up again, we're going to cut you loose and make sure you never work again."

Harry nodded. "I understand. I don't . . . It's hard to say no to someone from the past when the present feels wrong."

"What hold does he have on you?"

"He saved my life when I was young. I mean, really little, like six. A couple older boys were messing with me, and he came to the rescue. I didn't know his name or anything then."

"How did he know to contact you?"

"When he killed Armand, we saw each other. I knew he was that guy from the group home, and he remembered me. I guess he must have asked around about who we were. He contacted me two days ago, and I put him off, but then you were acting like a horny fool, and I thought we need the old Jack to catch this guy."

Horny fool. Yes, that was the image Jack wanted his men to have of him. "I've never lost my focus as leader of this team, Harry."

"I know that. It was my mistake to think the woman was the one making you weak."

"I'm not weak."

"I know that."

"Don't forget it."

"I won't," Harry said.

"Did you get any intel from Andreev regarding his location?"

"No. He was pretty terse in the messages, which came through the Savage Seven Web site."

"Man, he has some nerve thinking he can use our own resources against us. I don't want that to ever happen again, Harry. You made us all look like chumps."

"I know. I'm more sorry than I can say."

"I think you'll have a few bruises to remind you not to screw up again."

"Indeed. I already do."

The morning was starting to heat up in the hangar as they rejoined the rest of the team.

"Harry, would you mind contacting Andreev again?" Anna asked when they returned.

"Why?" Jack asked.

"Well, we've been talking, and if we're able to track the signal Andreev is using, we might be able to pinpoint his location. The Ahaggar Mountain range is vast and full of craters and caves. It could save us some time."

Jack nodded at the team. "Good idea."

"I can try to reach him, but if these guys go back to him, he'll know he's been compromised," Harry said.

Bay came forward from his place away from the group. "I know of some men who can hold the men for a month or so."

"But—" Anna said.

"No buts. That sounds good, Bay. Make that happen," Jack said.

"I will."

Harry turned to Anna. "What do you need me to do?"

"Well, can you contact him by phone?"

"I haven't. But he sent me an IM message this morning."

"Okay," Anna said. "Let me see your device, and then maybe together Tommy and I can come up with a Trojan-horse-type program that will let us into his system."

Tommy, Anna, and Harry went over to a small table and worked at the computer while Bay, Justine, and J.P. took the surviving Berbers to Bay's friends. They decided to leave the deceased in the hangar. Charity would place a call to the local authorities once they were out of the area.

Jack didn't like what had happened today, but he felt it had created a bond between his team and the Liberty Investigations gals. In a way it had made them into one team.

There would be no more dividing by sex or doing things in the "same old way" they had always done before.

Change was important—he knew that—and almost losing Harry the way they had cemented them together in a way only combat by fire could.

Chapter Sixteen

Jack didn't kid himself that Anna was going to welcome him into her room this night. So when they arrived at Tamanrasset and the team all headed up to their rooms for the night, he went to his. He had been in contact with Kirk, and the other man was now in the Ahaggar Mountains. Kirk would have a location for them to use in the morning.

Anna and Tommy had narrowed Andreev's location to a fifty-mile area. It wasn't as close as Jack would have liked, but it was close enough that they shouldn't need to spend too long stumbling blindly through the caves looking for Andreev.

There was a rap on his door, and he got up to see who it was. Anna stood there in the hallway. "You missed dinner."

"I did," he acknowledged. He'd had enough of everyone and had wanted to be alone to think about the way Anna had looked at him after the team had taken their revenge on Harry.

"Why?"

He shrugged. "It doesn't matter. What are you doing here?"

"I missed you."

"You did? Even though I'm a savage?"

"Yes, even though. It's hard for me to explain, but I like

the fact that you're the biggest badass out there. Yet at the same time I wish you could be a bit more civilized."

"I can't be. Even before I was Jack Savage, I wasn't a civil man."

"Who were you, Jack?" she asked. "Please trust me with your past."

"I will if you do."

"What's that mean?"

"Tell me about your kidnapping. You said it was someone you knew," he said. He drew her over to the bed and sat down. He wanted to hold her, and when she didn't pull away, he put his gun on the nightstand and drew her into his arms.

She took a deep breath. "Yes, it was someone I knew. Pierre Andre. He'd been stationed at an embassy with us before, and he had a daughter my age. But Amelia wasn't with him in Algiers, and he often would give me letters from her. We were pen pals—or so I thought. Eventually Pierre started writing the letters in Amelia's name."

Jack listened to her story and felt the rage build in him. He wanted to protect the innocent girl Anna had been. "What kind of man manipulates a child?"

"I don't know. But I did find out later that his daughter was being held by the same people who eventually took me. He had to turn me over to them to get Amelia free."

"Doesn't seem fair."

"Little in life is," she said. "Anyway, he took me to a group of Turkish militants. They wanted the British government to release several prisoners that were terrorists. And they thought my father would help them with that if they held me hostage."

"But he couldn't," Jack said.

"Exactly. I do know my dad aged twenty years in those

ten days I was gone. He was never the same again. My brother says dad had lost his faith."

"Faith in what?"

"In people. Being an ambassador, he'd always believed in a certain goodness in all people—that people needed to communicate and know each other's cultures. But my kidnapping changed him.

"I was kept for ten days, and Father had the SAS and some Algerian nationals looking for me. The Tuareg were the ones who found me first."

"What did that do to you?"

"The kidnapping?" she asked, tipping her head toward him.

He nodded.

"It made me who I am. I mean, I'm serious when it comes to protecting myself. That's why I get information. If I'd known Amelia wasn't at boarding school, I would have known to be suspicious of her father."

Jack doubted that. It was only in looking back that she thought she would have behaved differently, but he knew from experience that you seldom changed your behavior until the world changed you.

"I'm sorry, angel."

She turned her head and dropped a kiss on his chest. "Thanks for caring."

He held her for a few moments, stroking her arm and trying to think how to tell her his past wasn't something she would be able to stomach. "I can't tell you about my past, angel."

"Why not? I'll keep your secrets safe."

"I wasn't a nice man. And what you saw today with Harry—remember how that outraged you and made you upset with me?"

"Yes. But I think I've come to realize you're the kind of man you have to be. Please tell me. I won't overreact."

"It's not a question of overreacting. I don't want to tell you, because it might change the way you look at me. And I like it that you think I'm the biggest badass out there."

Anna smiled up at him. She really was the most beautiful woman he'd ever held. "I doubt a few dirty deeds are going to change my mind."

"Trust me. Some of the things I did make the devil look like a Sunday-school teacher."

"What were you?" she asked.

He tucked her head against his chest and whispered that he had been in black ops and that he'd organized coups and done the US government's dirty work until they'd decided he'd outlived his usefulness. He talked for a half hour of all the gruesome missions he'd been on.

"Oh, Jack. I'm so sorry you were used like that," Anna said. Inside she was shaking, trying to reconcile the man she had come to know with the monster he'd just described.

"It was a long time ago," he said, his voice deep.

Not long enough, Anna thought. Traces of that violent man still existed beneath the surface of Jack today. "I wish I could make that up to you," she said.

"You do whenever I hold you in my arms."

She was humbled by his words. And forced herself to shake off her own lingering doubts about his past actions. She knew she wasn't a femme fatale or supersexy woman, but with Jack she always felt that way. Twice he'd made love to her, and both times he'd made her feel as if she were something more than just Anna Sterling.

She leaned over and kissed him. The sting of his five-o'clock stubble was rough against her skin. She wrapped her legs around his hips as he rolled over until he was on top of her.

"I wanted to be on top," she said.

"Not this time, baby," he said with a wicked grin, lowering his body over hers.

"I want to explore you," she said. "Take off your shirt."

He did as she asked. "Now you do the same."

She took her blouse off slowly, enjoying the way his eyes narrowed when she revealed her breasts.

"I love your breasts," he said.

"Do you?"

His torso was hard with musculature as he rotated his shoulders. The light dusting of hair on his chest abraded her nipples.

Anna traced her fingers down Jack's bare back. He was hot, and sweat dotted his skin, especially at the small of his back. She drew her fingers through the dampness, pushing her fingers lower under the fabric of his pants.

He reached between their bodies and unfastened his pants and hers. She slid her hands lower until she cupped his butt.

His touch moved over her breasts, rubbing circles around the full globes but not touching her nipples, which tightened in anticipation. Leaning back on his legs, he knelt between hers, tweaking both of her nipples and then skimming his hands over her stomach. He explored every inch of her body, watching her carefully to see where she reacted.

"Lower," she said.

"Not yet. I want to take my time tonight."

She reached out and stopped his hand from moving. He gave her a hard look, his blue eyes diamond hard with warning. She knew then that any illusions she might have harbored of being in charge were false. He captured her hands, drawing them above her head.

She couldn't think as he thrust his tongue deep into her mouth and then lifted his head, biting at her bottom lip. He drew his hands down her arms and then slowly down her entire body, pulling her pants from her body and her shoes from her feet. She was left lying on the bed with her arms above her head wearing only her tiny, lacy thong underwear.

Anna felt so exposed as he stood at the end of the bed, slowly drawing his belt from the loops on his pants and then pushing his pants and underwear down his body in one long movement.

His cock was fully erect. He ran his hands down his own body, taking his cock in his hand and stroking it a few times. She saw a drop of pre-cum glistening on the edge of his erection, and she licked her lips, wanting to know the taste of him.

She pulled her hands away from the headboard and came up on her knees, crawling toward him. She put her hand over his, rubbing at the moisture there, taking it on her finger and bringing to her mouth.

He growled deep in his throat and lifted her off the bed. He sank down on the mattress, pulling her astride him, his mouth finding hers. Their tongues tangled, and she felt overwhelmed by him as his hands roamed all over her body, his fingers rubbing and caressing every inch of her skin while he made love to her with his mouth.

"Kneel up for me, honey," Jack said in a raspy voice that sent shivers coursing through her body.

Anna knelt with one leg on either side of his hips. He wrapped his arms around her, and his mouth latched on to her nipple, suckling her strongly.

She gasped his name. Humid warmth pooled in the center of her body, and she rocked against him, feeling the tip of his penis against her center. She wanted more. She needed him deep inside her. She needed it now.

She ached for his penetration. This was nothing like the

sexual encounters they had had before. It was more intense, more real, and probably because they'd both come so close to dying. She forced down the emotions that threatened to surface and focused only on the physical.

His cock was hot, hard, and ready between their bodies. She rocked against him, finding her own pleasure as he continued to lick and suck at her breasts. He held her butt in his big hands, controlling the movements of her hips. Falling backward on the bed, he took her with him, his mouth never leaving her skin.

He rolled her beneath him and explored her entire body, skimming his way down her sides, exploring every inch of her skin. She felt raw and exposed—wanted to reach for him and turn the tables, but she couldn't. His hands and mouth were everywhere, turning her on and making her crave more of his touch.

Anna laughed and jerked in Jack's arms as he found her ticklish spots. He moved farther down her body.

His hair was silky smooth against her stomach as he licked the area around her belly button and then put his tongue in. She arched off the bed, her hips trying to rise, but his hands on her thighs held her still.

He put his face right on top of her mons, resting his chin lightly on top of her clitoris and looking up at her. She wanted him so badly. Wanted to feel his mouth on her and his tongue and fingers inside her.

"Jack?"

"Hmmm?" he said, turning his head from side to side, caressing her with his entire face.

"Please . . ."

He moved back up over her body, stretching her arms over her head again. She gripped the headboard on her own. He moved his body over hers in one big caress that brought every one of her senses to hypersensitivity. She wanted him.

She couldn't take any more of this slow buildup to passion. She wrapped her legs around his waist and tried to impale herself on his cock, but he pulled back.

He nibbled his way down to the center of her body, squeezing her breasts against his face as he continued straight back to her aching center.

She parted her legs, opening them widely for him, and he lowered his head, taking her in his mouth. First his warm breath caressed her, and then his tongue. His fingers teased the opening of her body, circling but not entering her as his tongue tapped out a rhythm against her clit.

She gripped the headboard tighter and tighter as her hips rose and fell, trying to force him to penetrate her, but still he held his touch only at the entrance of her body.

"Please, Jack. I need you. Now."

He caught her clit between his lips and sucked her into his mouth at the same time that he thrust his finger deep into her body. She screamed as her body spasmed. She rocked her hips against his finger and mouth as he kept up the pressure, not letting her come down from her orgasm but building her up once again.

After she'd come down, Jack moved slowly up and over Anna. He was aching hard and needed to feel the silky smoothness of her pussy around him. She tunneled her fingers through his hair and pulled his mouth to hers. She was languid as she moved against him, her legs tangling with his.

Her hands swept up and down his back, sliding around his hip to find his hard-on, and stroked. She reached lower, cupping his balls in her hand, rolling them over her fingers, and he got so tight and so fucking hard he thought he was going to come before he could get inside her.

"Too much," he said, drawing her hand away. "I want to be inside of you now."

"I want that, too."

She wrapped her arms around him. He loved the feel of her long, cool fingers on him. When she found the sensitive area at the base of his spine, tracing her finger in a small circle, awareness spread up his body in waves, and a shudder went through his entire body.

Jack drew her hand away from his body and linked their fingers together, tasting her with long, slow sweeps of his tongue against her neck and collarbone. She smelled heavenly . . . of sex and woman—his woman.

He lifted himself away from her, kneeling between her legs. She touched his thigh—the only part of his body she could reach. Her fingers moved up his thigh and around to his hip, finding the scars that life had left on his body. Anna caressed them all. With her it didn't seem to matter that he was a battered warrior. With her he felt like he'd found the home, the sanctuary, he'd always been searching for.

She sat up, still caressing the scar that had been left by shrapnel. She glanced up at him, a question in her eyes. "Did you get this when you were the USA's bogeyman?"

He nodded. Before he could say anything else, she had lowered her head, her tongue tracing the rough skin, each of the peaks and valleys where the metal had dug into his body and branded him. Her hair was silky and cool against his lower body.

She nibbled on his hipbone and then tongued her way across his stomach, finding his belly button. She grazed her teeth lightly over his skin. Her fingers spread wide, caressing his entire body.

"Lie back on the bed. I want to make love to you," she said, her words spoken directly against his flesh. "So that you never forget me."

"Another time," he said, his voice low and guttural with need.

Jack cupped the back of Anna's head and drew her up his body. She licked and caressed him, lingering over his nipples, kissing and sucking them into her mouth one at a time, using her fingernail to abrade the one her mouth wasn't on.

His entire being ached to be buried in her. He didn't want to wait another second. Couldn't wait another second to get inside her. He tumbled her back on the bed. She held his shoulders as he slid up over her.

He tested her body to make sure she was still ready for him. He held his cock poised at her entrance. Felt her silky legs draw up his and then fall open. He held himself over her, less than an inch of space between their bodies, and waited. Anticipation made the base of his spine tingle.

Anna shifted under him, her shoulders rotating until the tips of her berry-hard breasts brushed against him. Her white-hot center brushed over his now condom-covered cock, and he wished they were flesh to flesh. He wanted to feel every inch of her.

He lowered himself over her, settling into place between her legs. She skimmed her gaze over his body down to the place where they met.

He lifted her hips and waited until her eyes met his, and then he slid into her body. She was always a tight fit, and he took her slowly, inch by inch, until he was fully seated inside her.

Anna closed her eyes for a minute, her arms closing so tightly around Jack he couldn't breathe—he couldn't breathe anyway as he started to move over her. Found her mouth with his. She turned her head away from him. Kissed his shoulders and his neck. Scraped her nails down his back as he thrust slowly, building them both toward the pinnacle.

He caught her face in his hand, tipped her head back until she was forced to look at him as he rode her. Her eyes widened, and he felt something change deep within him. She lifted her legs, wrapping them around his waist, and he slid a little deeper in her body, but not as deep as he wanted to be. He wanted to go so deep the two of them would never be separated again.

She gasped his name as he increased his pace, feeling his own climax rushing toward him. He changed the angle of his penetration so the tip of his cock would hit her G-spot.

Anna shifted around on him, grabbed a pillow, and wedged it under her hips; then she wedged a second one so he could kneel between her legs still thrusting. He could go deeper this way. Her eyes widened, her nails digging into his sides and then holding as her mouth opened on a scream that was his name as her orgasm rolled through her body. He continued thrusting, driving himself deeper and deeper until his balls tightened, drawing up against his body, and he came in a rush.

Jack fell to the side next to her, pulling her into his arms as the sweat dried on his body. Her head rested against his chest, and he swept his hands up and down, unable to stop caressing.

When their heartbeats slowed to something close to normal, he tipped Anna's head back and kissed her. He wondered if she'd admit that things had changed between them.

He went into the bathroom to take care of his mess and brought a damp washcloth back to clean her up as well. She said nothing as he tended to her, and then he tossed the washcloth on the floor and pulled her back into his arms.

Anna leaned up over him. There was a sadness in her eyes he didn't trust, and he had no idea what to do with her. "Why so sad?"

"I just realized tomorrow will change everything. We aren't going to be alone again."

"No, we aren't. At least not while we're here in Algeria. But we can . . ." He didn't finish that thought. They weren't going to get together once they got back to the States. He had his life in Florida, and she was a high-society girl in DC.

"I . . . I'm sorry for everything you've been through," Anna said.

"Me, too, angel. For tonight, will you stay with me and let me pretend we both aren't the scarred people we are?"

"No."

Jack sighed and sat up to hand her clothing to her, but she stopped him with her hand in the small of his back. "I'm not leaving. I just don't want to pretend we're someone else. I think I like you because of how my life shaped me. And I think it's the same for you."

The wisdom of that comment shouldn't have moved him, but it did. And it reminded him of just how much he cared for Anna Sterling.

Chapter Seventeen

Morning was cool in Tamanrasset, but it was a bit warmer than it had been in Algiers. Bay had informed them they could expect the same temperatures year-round in this region. And because they wouldn't be journeying into the Sahara, weather wasn't much of a concern. The Ahaggar Mountains didn't get a lot of rain.

Transportation was hard to find when they entered the city. They could take the Humvee and Land Rover into the mountains, but the roads weren't the best, and traveling would be difficult.

Bay thought they'd be fine with the four-wheel-drive vehicles. Kirk still hadn't checked in, but they had an idea of where to start looking for Andreev.

It was a basic route off the Assekrem circuit. They could join the few hearty souls who had journeyed up into Algeria from Mali.

Jack caught his breath as he stared at the bleak desert that lined one side of Tamanrasset—the Navel of the Sahara was a beautiful place. It was a shame that the unrest in Algeria kept this place from more people. But he knew the unspoiled beauty of the land would quickly disappear if tourism were easier.

In the stillness of the early morning they were the only ones moving around. The smell of the thick black coffee they had been served at their hotel was on the air. The women talked in a small group to the left of the vehicles, and the Savage Seven were standing off to the other side.

"Ready to head out?" Jack asked. He was too much a natural leader not to try to take charge, and he did it with ease.

"I think we are," Anna said. She had the program with the GPS location for Andreev's approximate location in her BlackBerry, though they didn't know how long the satellite would be available to them. Right now they could use it to guide them. "Charity is going to ride with Hamm, Tommy, J.P., and Harry. You're with me, Bay, and Justine," she said to Jack.

"Am I?" he asked.

"Yes. We wanted to make sure we had enough firepower spread between the two vehicles. And Tommy and I both have the same coordinates in our mobiles. That way, if anything happens, we're all covered."

This was the part of a mission Anna liked the best. There was something about putting on black leather pants and her holster she always enjoyed. She had her wireless radio in her ear and more weapons and gadgets strapped to her body than most people ever held.

Charity looked like a goth Barbie doll in her dark clothes. Anna knew all the women from Liberty were armed to the teeth. Justine had even loaded a bunch of extra weapons into the back of the Land Rover. She had seen Hamm do the same to the Humvee.

Jack looked breathtakingly handsome in the early morning light. She'd enjoyed spending the previous night with him so much. She only hoped it had meant something to him as well.

Knowing they both weren't used to that level of intimacy

on a mission reassured her. She was afraid for him but knew he'd survived a long time. She doubted he'd let Andreev get the better of him.

"We'll take the lead. Follow us. As soon as I hear from Kirk, I'll pass the information on to you."

"Sounds good," Charity said.

"Don't forget we want Andreev alive. We need to get access to his contacts and his client base," Anna said. She didn't trust the men not to enact a little vigilante justice when they saw Andreev.

"Everyone is aware of that," Jack said. "I know Armand is on my team's minds, but let's make sure we honor the good man he was by putting the job first. Armand would want that from us."

"We'll get the bastard," J.P. said. "He just has to be breathing to testify."

"No one lays a hand on him unless I say so," Jack told his men sternly.

"Yes, sir," they all answered at once.

They all manned up into their vehicles, and as they pulled out in front of the Humvee, Anna realized she was again going into an unknown situation with someone other than just Justine and Charity at her back. She wasn't sure what she expected, but it was going to be different.

"This is the strangest op," Justine said.

"I've never been in a group like this before," Bay said.

"Do you have a problem with women?" Justine asked.

"No. My people are matriarchal. We know the strength of women."

"Good. I already liked you, but now I really like you," Justine said.

Anna had to laugh at that, and soon she heard Jack join in. It was probably just that they were heading into a dangerous situation with an adversary that had manpower they weren't sure of. It was the release they needed before they got too far up the brown and yellow mountains. Because then the tension would start to grow, and they'd all be on a knife's edge, as they should have been.

"I wouldn't have put this team together on my own," Jack said. "But it makes a certain sense when we're all together. Andreev isn't going to know what hit him."

"Good. Then we can capture him like we should have done back in Seattle," Anna said. It seemed like a lifetime ago when she'd made the connection between the embezzler at AlberTron and the weapons dealer every nation wanted out of business.

Jack drove through the rugged terrain listening with one ear to the directions Anna gave. He couldn't get the previous night out of his head. He wanted to take Anna and hide away from the world. Which was a marked difference from the man he'd always been.

He hadn't really let the government shape him into a killing machine—he'd insisted they do it. He'd liked the fact that he was the best they had. The go-to guy when there was a problem diplomacy wouldn't fix.

It wasn't lost on him that Anna came from a background on the opposite side of the coin.

She looked hot as hell in those black leather pants and the molded zip-front leather jacket. The women of Liberty Investigations would give most men an instant hard-on if they saw them together.

But Anna was more than a sexy woman to Jack. He knew she wore the leather for the protection it offered. He had seen her in action yesterday at the hangar, and he knew she was capable of handling the weapons she wore.

She winked at him, and he knew she'd caught him staring. He just shrugged. He liked seeing her like this. Being with her. How the hell was he going to handle his next op? After working so closely with Anna, it was going to seem . . . wrong, he imagined.

Bay sighed as soon as they left the city.

"What are you thinking, Bay?" Anna asked.

"That it is good to be home. I like my job working for Interpol, but I do miss these mountains and my people."

"I always feel the same way about DC and London," Anna said.

"You have two homes?"

"London is where my mother and brother are, so it's the home I remember from my childhood. And DC is my home now, so it's welcoming in an entirely different way."

"I can understand that. You aren't tied to the land the way I am."

"Tied in what way?" Jack asked.

"By my soul. I don't sleep as well when I'm away for too long."

Jack had heard a lot about the mysticism of the Tuareg and had experienced a little of it when he and Bay had gone into that lodge in El Golea, but this was the first time he'd ever really talked to the other man. And a part of him envied Bay.

Because Bay wasn't talking about home as a dwelling you returned to. Bay was talking about home as a *belonging*, and Jack knew he'd never had a place like that.

Well, he'd felt something close to it when he'd held Anna in his arms, but he doubted a person could be home. Could they?

"Where is your home, Justine?" Bay asked.

"I always thought it was DC, but Nigel and Piper are my home. Is that silly? To think that a person is?"

"No," Bay said.

Jack didn't say anything. He thought sometimes it was a little eerie how similar he and Justine were. He knew little of her past, but he wouldn't be surprised if she'd come from a broken home like he had.

"Who's Nigel?"

"My fiancé. I . . . I'm recently engaged. He's a nice guy, not a creep or anything."

Jack almost laughed at the way Justine spoke. But he didn't. He could tell from her words that she must sometimes still feel like some kind of weird miracle had happened to bring her Nigel.

"My wife and children live in Djanet," Bay said. "They are as much my home as this place is. Jack, where is your home? DC?"

"No. I'm from Florida. I have a place in Arlington, but I really don't feel like I'm home until I'm back at the little beach house that was my grandfather's."

"Do you have anyone special waiting for you?" Bay asked.

Jack wanted to glance at Anna but knew this wasn't the time to find out how she felt about him thinking she was the most important person in his life.

"I have a dog my neighbor watches while I'm gone," Jack said at last.

"It's good to have animals around us. Some cultures believe they're spirit guides."

"Well, this dog is lazy and doesn't do anything but sit on my front porch and eat me out of house and home."

Justine laughed, but Anna didn't, and he wondered what she was thinking. Maybe she was wondering why he had only a dog waiting for him at home. Or maybe she had already surmised that he was the kind of man who didn't really connect too well with other people.

"I'm pretty much a loner," Jack said and then did glance

over at Anna. "Sometimes I meet someone who makes a difference in my life."

Anna tilted her head to one side. "Me, too."

"Anna isn't a loner. That girl knows someone everywhere we go," Justine said.

"I might know people, but that doesn't mean I don't feel alone."

Jack nodded at her. They had a connection, and he only hoped he could complete this mission without doing anything that would really frighten her off, because his behavior with Harry had been tame. He knew inside was a real savage waiting to get out, and he knew Andreev was the man who could bring that savage to the surface.

"I can see why you love this place, Bay. It's very beautiful in a stark way," Anna said.

"It's also a very dangerous place, so I've always respected the land."

"Do you mean men?" Jack asked.

"Men sometimes. But I meant the sirocco."

"How often do they blow?" Anna asked. "I don't think we're prepared to deal with a hell wind on this trip."

Bay shrugged, and Jack felt a chill on his spine. "They blow when they need to."

"That doesn't sound very reassuring," Justine said. "Can we make a sacrifice to the gods and appease them?"

"I don't worship false gods, Justine. Only Allah." And that seemed to put a damper on everyone's spirits. Jack drove through the mountains wanting to find Andreev's camp so he could confront an enemy he knew how to fight.

Demetri got the news that three of his men had been reported missing minutes before the two men he'd hired to help with the weapons deal arrived. Kirk Mann looked like a cocky American, and because Demetri knew the Americans had killed his assassins, he was more than a little pissed off.

But Mann was a good man and always did what he was hired to do. And his buyers liked seeing a muscular man handling their weapons. It made them think the thirteen-year-old boys they gave the assault rifles might someday look like men trained to be war machines.

"Were you followed?" Andreev asked Mann.

"Not likely. This place is damned hard to find. If it hadn't been for Yan, I would have turned back."

"Good. That's as it should be. The weapons you'll be demonstrating are being held up that trail about fifteen kilometers. You can bunk up there."

"Whatever. It's colder here than I expected it to be," Kirk said.

"Its February, in case you forgot."

"Yeah, I know, but we're close to the desert."

Americans could be so stupid when it came to geography, Andreev thought. If he'd been this stupid, he wouldn't be the man he was today.

"The demonstration will be tomorrow. I want to have a run-through this afternoon so we're sure you can use all the weapons and there are no malfunctions when the clients are here."

"No problem. What am I handling?"

"Assault rifles and RPG launchers. Nothing too intense. I have some new ammo that will blow you away."

"Literally, right?" Kirk said.

"Yes. You may go now," Andreev said.

Demetri didn't like dealing with mercenaries. He had to because that was the nature of his business. And he didn't like to have regular men in his camp. But he had to find a different class of person to help him out.

He knew Mann was simply doing the job he was hired to do, but Andreev worried about how much loyalty one could buy for twenty-five thousand dollars. He didn't think it bought as much as it used to.

Andreev glanced over at Mann. He had to be very sure of every man in his camp. One screwup and the entire business he'd built would be ruined. Andreev looked the man in the eyes. Mann had been working as a gun-for-hire for more than ten years. And he had no doubt Mann would never back down if confronted by an enemy. But he needed to know Mann would stand by his side.

"Are you sure you need me?" Kirk asked. "You seem at home with weapons."

"What do you mean?" Andreev asked, holding his gun easily at his side. Casually he removed a cloth from the desk behind him. He folded the scarflike garment into the right size and density for a silencer.

Mann turned his back to Andreev, and Andreev lifted the gun and the cloth. Mann glanced over his shoulder at Andreev, eyes widening and hands coming up in an *I surrender* gesture. Mann took a step back. "I wasn't saying I didn't want this gig. Just questioning if you needed me. I'm your guy. You've paid for my services, and they're yours."

Andreev continued to stare at Mann until beads of sweat dotted Mann's forehead. Then he lowered his gun, tucking it into the back of his pants.

"Make sure you remember that," Demetri said.

Mann nodded. Demetri would have to keep a close eye on him in case Mann decided to double-cross him.

But for now, Andreev noticed that Mann was focused on

getting to the weapons cache, and that was just what Andreev wanted. He like his men focused on the job. Because
men who weren't were sloppy. And sloppy men ended up
dead or in jail.

Andreev felt a surge of adrenaline. There was something
to be said about being back where he was truly himself. He
missed the family he had in the US, but there he had to
hide his temper and blend in with the other executives.
Here he could be the man he was always meant to be.

Andreev felt his determination to make this latest sale a
success just to thumb his nose at Liberty Investigations,
who'd ruined what he'd built.

"Yan?"

"Yes, sir?"

"Have you heard from our men yet? Did they take care of
the women?"

Yan fiddled nervously with his cell phone. "I'm not sure."

"What? Why not?"

"I got a short text message saying they had engaged the
women . . . then forty-five minutes later, another that said it
was over."

Demetri knew that wasn't proof, but the men he'd hired
were the best in the business. "Call them."

Yan dialed the number and a minute later the phone was
answered. In the quiet of the room he could hear the voice
on the other end. "Are they dead?" Yan asked.

"Yes."

Demetri smiled. He wanted to kill those women again.
He did feel a certain amount of pleasure when he thought
of them dead in that hangar in In Salah. That would teach
Sam Liberty to meddle where he wasn't supposed to
meddle.

Andreev didn't want trouble, but he was prepared for it.

Men like Mann had been bought once and could just as easily have sold him out.

"Yan?"

"Sir?"

"Follow him and make sure everything is set up for the demo this afternoon."

"Yes, sir."

"Where are the men you hired?"

"They're still at the cache," Yan said.

"Make sure someone stays with Mann at all times. I don't trust him."

"Yes, sir. I'll personally take the task. This is going to be the start of a new era for us, and I won't let anything screw it up."

"See that you don't, Yan. I will reward you with more wealth than you can imagine."

Yan nodded and turned away. It was easier to buy men in this part of the world because wealth was still such a foreign concept. He could trust Yan, but Mann he'd have to be careful with.

He knew it was only a matter of time before he'd have to find men of his own. Men who worked for him for more than one mission—loyal men he could keep employed full time. Maybe after this deal he'd be in a better position to do so.

Chapter Eighteen

Kirk planted a GPS beacon at Andreev's base camp, and Anna picked it up shortly after noon. "We need to leave the vehicles and go on foot to the camp," she told her team.

"How far?"

"Probably not any more than five miles," Anna said, pointing. "That way."

"The terrain in that direction is tough to traverse. It will take at least three hours. But the weather looks nice," Bay said.

"Okay, we'll stop up ahead," Jack said.

"Charity?"

"Go ahead," Charity said on mic.

"We're stopping up ahead. Mann's GPS signal is coming through loud and clear. We're going to hike in."

"Affirmative. Have you had a chance to check the weather forecast?"

"Yes, we're clear. There's little cloud coverage. We should have nice weather all morning."

"Great. I'll pull in behind Savage. Charity out."

Anna was glad they were here. This had been the longest five days of her life, and she wanted Andreev out of the way, captured, and talking so she could figure out if there was something more between her and Jack than just red-hot sex.

Which had been nice, she thought, glancing at him through heavy-lidded eyes. He was earthy and sensual and made her feel more like a woman than she'd ever felt before.

Jack eased the vehicle onto the shoulder, and they all got out. "We aren't going to be able to take all the extra firepower unless one of you can carry it," he said.

"I don't think we'll need it," Anna said.

"We don't know how many men we'll be facing," Justine said. "We need to have at least one launcher and probably a couple AK-47s."

"I agree," Jack said. "I can carry an extra bag."

The Humvee stopped behind them, and Anna had a moment of unreality. Here they were in the Ahaggar Mountains, a place of infinite beauty, and they were about to do something very ugly. She had never thought of her job in terms like that, but that sense that she had been changing was continuing.

She wanted Andreev captured. She wanted illegal sales of arms and munitions to stop because she'd always believed— probably because of her father—that diplomacy was better for the people of the world than armed coups.

But as they manned up and double-checked their weapons, Anna saw that sometimes a show of force was the only way.

"Are you okay?" Jack asked.

She nodded her head. "Yes. I was just getting myself ready for this mission."

He nodded and then surprised her by leaning over and kissing her. "Stay safe, angel. I'm not done with you yet."

Before she could respond, he was off, following Bay down the path into the interior of the mountains. Justine was next, and Anna fell into step beside her friend. She checked her weapon and then her technology.

"This is a very different mountain range than Peru," Justine said.

"Yes, it is."

The GPS beacon continued to beep on Anna's Black-Berry. Justine wasn't a talker, and that didn't change now. They just kept moving in a rough single-file formation. The path, if it could be called that, didn't really allow for much side-by-side stuff.

When the path opened up again, Justine slowed her pace until she was next to Anna.

"How much longer do you think we have?" Justine asked.

"Another hour and a half."

"I hate this part of the mission. Get me in close where I can start using my weapons, and I'm a happy camper."

"Amen, sister," J.P. said behind them. "I hate hiking into an op. That's one nice thing about doing military work. They usually get you in closer."

"Yeah, but here? I don't think that would fly," Anna said. "There are a lot of wind currents on the mountains that would make a chopper hard to navigate."

"What about a plane? Parachute in?" J.P. asked.

"I guess. But we don't have one."

"I know. I just like to figure out different scenarios in my head."

"Why?" Anna asked.

"So I can make sure we aren't missing something obvi-ous. I mean, we think Andreev won't have another way out of the mountains, but what if he does?"

Anna considered that. There simply wasn't room on this type of path for any kind of large vehicle. "He could have a motorbike."

J.P. nodded. "If he does, I'll take it out."

She realized J.P.'s game with himself was simply an exercise in reassurance, in creating problems before he got into a situation, and in finding the solution.

She liked it and thought about the problems they were facing. But with this many men, she wasn't worried about Andreev. Despite the fact that he sold weapons for a living, he wasn't a big bad monster in her book. He was simply a man who'd escaped justice for too long, and she knew there was no way they were going to let him continue. She imagined that Jack and his team would kill Andreev if given the chance, and she knew she'd have to be on lookout to make sure they were able to bring Andreev into custody.

She wanted him captured because that was her mission objective, unlike the Savage Seven who wanted him captured because he'd actually gone after not one but two of their own.

Finally they made it to the base camp. Jack drew them to a halt at a spot overlooking the cave system. There were three vehicles and two motorbikes in the clearing. If they hadn't had seven of them working the square, Anna really would have been worried about Andreev slipping away. But as it was, her team members were all on and all wired. It was late afternoon, and there was plenty of light to see by.

"We need to split up," Charity said. "J.P. and Harry, take care of those vehicles. We don't want Andreev or any of his men escaping."

"Affirmative," J.P. said. And he and Harry moved swiftly away toward the cars. "We'll continue monitoring your channel."

"There are two main areas down there. It makes the

most sense if we work together. My guys and I will head toward the cave system to the left," Jack said.

"Okay, we'll handle the area to the right," Anna said. "Isn't it odd that there are no sentries?"

"Yes," Jack said. "Stay sharp and stay focused."

"Yes, sir," his team said, one by one, on the radio.

Anna had a new respect for Jack, watching him with his men. She might not always approve of the way he did business, but he did know how to command his troops.

"Be careful, Anna," Jack said in a whisper-soft tone, and she glanced over at him. She raised her hand to her lips and blew him a kiss before turning and walking away. She had a feeling in her gut that he was saying good-bye,

She switched frequencies on her earpiece and put it back in place. "Justine?"

"Right here, Anna."

"Did you put that bug in Jack's piece?" she asked.

"Yes, I did. Why are you asking?"

She shrugged her shoulders to loosen them under her leather jacket. The holster of her gun rested comfortably along the small of her back. Her leather pants were form-fitting and good for both protection from bullets and knives but also allowed her some fluidity if she had to use martial arts. "No reason. Just checking."

"I don't like this setup," Charity said. Their group moved in a loose formation. "I'll take the front."

"I've got you covered," Anna said. She kept her eyes sharp as Charity moved down the path toward the cave area. She didn't concentrate on Jack or his team. She knew they'd do their job.

She also wished liked hell they had some kind of heat image from this place so they knew how many men they were dealing with.

"Justine, you're clear."

"I'm moving. Anna, watch the back path."

"I am."

"I'm in," Charity said in a near-soundless voice. "There are two guards watching several crates that I can only assume have weapons in them. And the sentries are moving in ten-minute rotations."

Anna crossed to Justine's location, and together they used hand signals to move into the cave.

"Charity?"

"Behind the large cache of boxes."

"We're moving on three," Justine said.

But before they could take a step, Andreev entered from the back of the large, cavernous room. Anna signaled for Justine to wait.

"Were you followed?" Andreev asked in Arabic to someone the women couldn't see.

"I shouldn't have been. Tamanrasset was quiet this morning when I left. And it's not hard to watch my back trail," came a male voice.

Andreev was slimmer than Anna remembered him. But otherwise he was the same.

"Good. Then everything is in place?" Andreev asked.

"Yes, sir. The buyers will be here at first light."

Andreev turned, and Anna ducked back out of his line of sight.

"Should we wait?" Justine asked as Andreev and the man moved off.

"No. We aren't interested in his buyers, only in him," Charity said.

"Agreed," Anna said. "I think we should disarm these weapons and take out the guards. Is anyone else going to join us from the direction Andreev came?"

It was dark in the cave, and Anna finally felt her eyes adjust completely.

"I don't know. I'll secure the area back here," Charity said.

"We're on these two guards. We'll join you when this room is clean."

"I've got the one on the right," Justine said.

"Affirmative," Anna answered. "We move on three."

"Three, two, one."

Deliberately Anna stepped into the path of the guard closest to her. He pivoted toward her, raising his gun. She stepped toward him, grabbing his wrist right above where the meat of his thumb and wrist came together. Her hand didn't make it all the way around his large wrist. But she used forced to push his hand down. He punched her with his left hand, hitting her in the cheek. She hit him with a roundhouse kick to the gut. He snarled some curse words at her.

She didn't loosen her grip on his gun hand. Finally Anna was able to grab the gun by the barrel and pull it from his grasp. He jerked his arm away as she snagged his weapon. He came at her with a front snap kick aimed at her chin. She twisted to the left, and he hit her shoulder instead. It ached.

She'd had enough of this guy. Coming around behind him, she knocked him on the head with her gun hand. He grunted but didn't fall down. She grabbed his meaty neck and felt around for his carotid artery, hoping to put him out.

The guard elbowed her in the gut and turned on her. He gripped her neck with both hands, lifting her off her feet and closing his hands. She struggled for breath.

Lifting both of her feet against his chest, she pushed back with all her might, and he tightened his hands for a second before her leverage gave her the advantage and she broke free. He fell backward, and so did she, landing on her ass with a jarring impact.

She stood quickly, bringing the heel of her foot down on one of his hands and twisting the other one behind his back. Anna forced him to roll over, and then she bound his wrists and feet. "One guard down."

"Mine, too. Let's find Charity and then go after Andreev."

Jack hoped Kirk wasn't incapacitated, but because they hadn't heard from him, Jack had to assume that was the case.

It was time for their briefing before the men moved forward with their mission. He also had to make sure they understood the ROEs. Jack didn't want his guys going Rambo on Andreev.

"We'll go in quiet and quick. There are four targets," Jack said, restating their mission objective for Tommy and Hamm. "Tommy, you will provide cover from here." He indicated a small ridge less than fifty feet from the main cave.

"Hamm, how many sentries did you observe?" Jack asked. He'd had Hamm keeping watch while the snipers had been scouting for a good location to set up.

"A two-man unit, sir. They're making rounds every forty minutes. We should be able to slip by them without notice."

"I think we should take them out. So we don't have to worry about them," J.P. said, joining them.

"The vehicles are inoperable," Harry said.

"Good."

Jack felt the tension in this group. They wanted their team members back together, and he knew they were ready for blood. They'd been waiting too long for action, and now they were ready to move.

"Agreed. We'll take the sentries on the way in." The smoother and quicker they could get this done, the better it would be for all involved. "We're going in soft. You need a confirmation before you make a kill. Is that understood?"

"Yes, sir."

"Let's check our radios, and then we'll move out." Jack waited until he was sure each man had placed the earbud in his ear.

"This is one," Jack said.

"Two," J.P. said.

"Three," Hamm said.

"Four," Harry said.

"Five," Tommy said.

"We'll be on silent until we reach the target. J.P., I want you to come in from the north side and take care of the sentry patrolling on that side. Hamm, you cover us from the west. Tommy and Harry, you'll take the east. Cover the path leading into the cave. I'll take out the guard on the south side. Let's move out."

The men fanned out in the area surrounding the cave. The afternoon sunlight gave them too much exposure to just maneuver closer. They were on silent maneuvers. They were all on their bellies inching their way closer to the cave.

A small chirping sounded in Jack's ear, and he acknowledged the signal from Anna's team that they were in position and handling their part of the mission.

Jack shifted to his knees as one of the sentries neared his position. He used the mountain terrain and underbrush for cover. He saw Hamm out of the corner of his eye, but Jack signaled him that he could handle the guard on his own.

Jack came up from his knees, wrapping one arm around the guard's throat. The guard wrapped his hands around

Jack's wrist and tossed him over his shoulder. Jack came up
in a rolling movement, getting his feet under him and finding his balance. The guard moved toward him with a roundhouse punch to the head. Jack turned his body to the left,
bringing his left arm up to block.

He connected with the guard's jaw with a solid right
hook. Then he twisted his left arm around the guard's right,
grasping his wrist and pulling him forward while he used his
right hand to give a palm strike to the guard's nose. Blood
gushed from the man's face as he lashed out with a strong
front snap kick.

Jack deflected the blow with his thigh and spun back
away from the guard, lashing out with a crescent kick that
caught the guard squarely on the side of the head. The
guard took a step backward, reaching for his weapon.

Jack grabbed the guard's hand, pulling him toward him
and hitting him in the side with a hammer fist right above
his ribs. The guard grunted and tried to kick him, but Jack
used his grip on the man's arm to force him to the ground.

The man dropped to his knees, and Jack got him in a
chokehold, cutting off his air. When the man went limp in
his arms, Jack bound his hands behind his back with a zip
cord and then did the same to his feet. He used a piece of
duct tape over his mouth to keep him from raising the alarm
if he came to.

Then he dragged the man deeper into the brush and continued moving forward to the cave. Each man chirped softly
when they were in position. Jack collected his thoughts. He
wanted Andreev, and so far they'd had no visual on the bastard.

"Anna?"

"Yes?"

"Have you seen Andreev?"

"He's out of the cave. I'm not sure where. We just handled two guards here. There's an office of some sort in the back. I'm going to check his computer for information, and Charity and Justine are going after Andreev."

"Negative. Have them stay with you. I don't want you alone."

"I can handle myself, Jack. I'm a big girl."

"Are you a big girl?" Andreev's voice came over Jack's radio.

"Yes, Demetri, I am," Anna said.

Jack cursed. "Don't antagonize him."

"Too late," Anna said.

Jack turned to his team, but they had heard the exchange as well. They all moved quickly toward the other cave area.

Chapter Nineteen

Liberty Investigations really pissed Demetri off. Why wouldn't these women die and stay dead?

He knew the problem was that he had sent another man to do a job he should have done.

He couldn't believe Anna was in his office going through his computer. He didn't see any type of flash drive in her hands, but he had no idea how long she'd been in here.

He'd moved quickly and, staying to the shadows, crept up behind her. Before she could turn, he'd grabbed the back of her jacket at the base of her neck with his left hand. She'd shrugged in his grip, lashing backward with a strong kick that connected with his thigh.

"Where are your girlfriends?" he asked.

"Let me go."

"I don't think so."

He brought his right hand across her throat, trying to subdue further assault, but she twisted in his grip, bringing her heel down on his instep.

Andreev tightened his grip on her throat, closing off her airway. She went limp in his arms, her slight body slumping in his arms. He started to loosen his grip, but she twisted against him. He put his left hand on her forehead, securing her in a headlock and pulling her backward to force her off balance.

She screamed again, and he put his palm over her mouth and nose. "If you don't want to die, shut up."

Her eyes widened, connecting with his. He stepped back and went down on his left knee, keeping the headlock secure. She reached up, gouging her nails across his face. He brought his right leg over her left arm and pulled it back to restrain her.

Anna just dug her nails into his lower calf. Her fingers scored the skin through the fabric of his pants. She flailed in his arms until he leaned forward, using his body weight to bring her under control. He rolled her onto her stomach, keeping the headlock secure. He let go of her forehead and pulled her hands together behind her back.

Andreev used his belt to bind her hands behind her back. Then he took his handkerchief from his pocket and stuffed it in her mouth.

He pulled her to her feet, gathered up her bag, and pulled her down the hallway. Where Yan waited. "Get rid of her."

Yan tossed Anna over his shoulder, and Andreev double-checked to make sure his computer information hadn't been breached. "We've got company," Andreev said.

"What should I do with the girl? Kill her?"

"No. Just toss her someplace where we won't have to worry about her. There are two other women around here as well. We need to find them and make sure they don't interfere more than they already have."

Andreev pulled his Glock from his holster and double-checked the clip. His face ached from where Anna had scratched it. What a bitch. He really hated dealing with people like the ones in Liberty Investigations.

Life was much nicer when he was alone in his part of the

world. He could understand them coming after him in Seattle, but here?

They were in his world now, and he wasn't going to pull any punches. "I want to finish this," he said.

"I'm with you, sir. Mann is in the other room. Two of our guards have been knocked out."

"Mann!" Andreev yelled.

Mann appeared in the doorway. "I can't revive your guards."

"Don't worry about them. I want you to go find the other two women and take them out."

"Kill them?"

"Yes. Is that a problem?"

Mann shrugged. "Not really, but you didn't pay me for that."

"I'll pay you double what I promised for the weapons demo. Just get out there and take care of them. I have clients coming this afternoon, and I want this place secure."

"No problem."

Andreev followed Mann into the other room. Yan left Anna in the office bound and gagged.

How had this happened? No one had found his base of operations in all the years he'd been operating. He should ask the woman some questions.

"Follow Mann and make sure that there isn't anyone in the camp," Andreev ordered Yan. "Wake up," he commanded Anna.

She moaned a little and opened her eyes.

"How did you find me?" he asked her.

She shook her head and moved her mouth. He reached down and removed the gag.

"I tracked your mobile phone," she said.

"I threw away my phone from America in Paris."

"We aren't without means. We work with a number of government agencies. You were on a commercial flight from Paris to Morocco. It didn't take a genius to figure out you'd be going someplace that was hard for us to follow."

"Yes, but these mountains. How did you know to look here?"

"I've got good instincts," she said.

He knew she was lying to him. He reached over and grabbed her hair, pulling her head back. "I don't like being lied to."

She jerked her head free of his grip. "I don't like bastards who think they are above the law."

"I'm not above the law, Anna. I'm outside of it."

"Not anymore," a man said from behind him.

Andreev turned to see Jack Savage and knew his day wasn't going to get any better.

Jack drew his Sig Sauer as he eased up on Andreev. The bastard was going to die. Jack didn't care what the ROEs or the mission specs were.

Andreev glanced at Jack in full desert camouflage. Then he looked at Anna.

"I will kill the woman," Andreev said.

"You don't want to kill me, Demetri. You aren't a murderer."

"I certainly don't want to die, and that's what this man has on his mind."

"You don't have to kill anyone. We're only here to arrest you," Anna said.

"I'm not going to jail. I saw what that did to my brother."

"Suits me," Jack said. He didn't like letting someone like Andreev off scot-free, and going to jail would hardly make up for all the lives Andreev was directly responsible for taking. If this man hadn't sold weapons to militant groups . . . well, Jack might have been out of work.

Andreev was distracted by Anna. Jack moved quickly to Andreev's right side and turned sideways. Leading with his left foot, he stepped diagonally toward Andreev, keeping his shooting arm directly in front of him. He grabbed Andreev's wrist with his left hand, bringing his weapon up toward Andreev's face.

Andreev brought his left hand up in a crosscut punch that knocked Jack's head back. Jack held tight to Andreev's wrist, and the other man hit him again, pivoting on his left foot and breaking Jack's grip on his arm.

"Don't move, or you're next," Andreev said, bringing out his weapon. Jack was in point-blank range. Jack took two steps backward, bringing his handgun up.

"How good a shot are you, Andreev?" Jack asked.

"Yan!" Andreev called. "Get your ass in here!"

Yan appeared, weaponless and surprised, at the door. Jack included him in his line of fire.

"You killed one of our men. Armand Mitterand," Jack said to Demetri. "We've got you surrounded. There's no one coming to help. Drop your weapon and surrender."

"Surrender isn't an option," Andreev said and turned to look to Anna across the room. Yan was still standing there, watching the tableau between Jack and his boss.

Jack divided his attention between Anna and Andreev. Andreev had to know he wasn't getting out of this cave alive, or, if he did make it out, that he was going to jail for a long time.

Jack knew his men were working their way in, could hear the signals on the radio. But he had no idea how much time they had.

"Yan, get the girl. We will take her with us."

Jack pulled a second gun. "Stop, Yan. Or die."

The other man hesitated and then drew a gun from his holster. "Which one of us will die?"

"You," Jack said, firing his weapon and watching Yan fall to the floor. He saw the horror in Anna's eyes that he would kill someone at point-blank range. But this wasn't some kind of computer simulation, and unless he fired, they were both going to die.

Andreev turned his gun toward Anna and fired. The bullet hit her in the shoulder, and he heard her cry out in pain.

"Let me go, or she dies. I'm not going to discuss this at all."

But Anna suddenly pulled her hands free of her binds. The move startled the other man.

"I don't think it's Anna's day to die," Jack said.

Andreev turned toward him for a split second, which was all the opening Anna needed. She rose to her feet and let a knife fly across the room, hitting Andreev's gun arm and making him drop his weapon. It fell on the floor at his feet.

Jack went in low, kicking the weapon out of Andreev's reach. Andreev scrambled for his weapon. He palmed his gun and rolled to his feet, bringing his weapon up.

Jack fired, aiming for Andreev's gun hand. Andreev fired at the same instant. Jack turned sideways to present as small a target as possible and felt the bullet enter the fleshy part of his upper arm.

Anna charged Andreev, hitting him with a flying side kick that drove him to his knees. She spun around, out of reach of his good arm.

Jack approached from Andreev's left side, striking Andreev's right arm and bringing his body around with a circular motion. He took Andreev's elbow with his left hand and forced Andreev's hand toward the ground, not stopping until Andreev lay on the floor at his feet.

Jack forced Andreev over onto his stomach and brought both of his hands together behind his back, binding them with a zip cord from his pocket. His entire body ached from head to toe, but when Anna sank down next to him, her small arms wrapping around his waist, he felt a wave of peace wash over him.

He wanted to pound on Andreev. In the past he would have taken his aggression out on the man, but he wasn't that man anymore. Anna had changed him, and he was happy for it. He held her loosely in his arm. The smell of blood was thick in the air.

"I thought we were both going to die," she said.

"No way, angel. I finally found something worth living for. You think I'd give that up?"

"No, I guess you wouldn't."

"What happened in here?" Justine asked as she entered the office area.

"Where were you?"

"Um, taking care of the other guards and capturing the prime minister of Serbia. They were the client."

"Good job," Anna said.

Jack didn't give a crap about any of that stuff. He wanted to take Andreev into custody, and then he wanted to take Anna someplace where they could be alone. But that would have to wait. He let her go as his men came in. Hamm bandaged his shoulder, and when Jack looked around for Anna a few hours later, he saw she was gone.

A week later, Anna was back in DC. Her life had returned to normal . . . well, almost. Charity and Justine were both on leave for some well-deserved vacation. And Sam had told Anna he wasn't going to close the office, but maybe look at taking on less dangerous assignments. She didn't know what that meant, but it didn't sound like what she wanted from her life.

Hell, who was she kidding? She missed Jack, and nothing

at work was going to fill the gap of excitement he'd brought to her personal life.

"Need a ride?"

Jack was suddenly standing in the entryway of the office, his heavy overcoat dusted with the light snow that was falling. He looked tired, but otherwise she couldn't read any emotion on his face. He wasn't the Savage Seven operative she'd last seen in the Ahaggar Mountains.

Andreev had been arrested and was awaiting trial. His database of clients was being read by government agencies, and there was a worldwide effort to make sure the weapons he'd sold were recovered.

"Thanks," she said to him.

Jack slipped his arm around her shoulder and led her to his car. He opened the passenger's door for her, but before she could climb into the car, he took her in his arms. "Damnit, why haven't you called me?"

Anna held him as tightly as he held her. "Why haven't you?" She closed her eyes and just breathed in the scent of him, thankful that he was there with her and that she was in his strong arms.

"You scared the shit out of me," he said.

She slid her hands down his back and cupped his backside. "Sorry." She didn't want to let this get too serious. She didn't trust what she felt for Jack.

"I'm not kidding, Anna."

"I know."

"Every time I close my eyes I see you bound on the floor again, and this time you don't get up."

He made a rough sound deep in his throat and then lifted her face to his, kissing her deeply and holding her to him with a strength that would have frightened her a few weeks ago. But now it felt right that he should need her as desperately as she desired him.

"Come home with me. Let me make love to you so I can know we're really safe and that you're really mine."

Anna nodded. Jack hustled her into the car and drove them quickly to his Arlington apartment. He started kissing her in the elevator, his hands roaming up and down her body, leaving no part untouched. She did the same to him, understanding that these caresses were, for both of them, a way of confirming the other was alive and well.

Jack lifted her into his arms when the elevator stopped on his floor. He had the apartment door open in no time flat, slammed it closed behind them, and set her on her feet, backing her up against the wall as he pushed her coat to the floor and pulled her sweater over her head.

He unfastened her bra and shoved it down her arms. He palmed her breasts in both hands, his mouth sliding along her neck and biting her lightly at the base. She shivered, undulating against him. She grabbed his shoulders and encountered his heavy topcoat. She pushed at the fabric, finally forcing it off his shoulders. His hands left her breasts for a minute, and he tossed his coat aside and then ripped off his shirt.

She caressed the rippling muscles of his chest, tugging on the light patch of hair and scraping her fingernail over his flat nipples. He groaned her name and lifted her under her arms.

"Open your legs."

She did, and he forced himself between them. His mouth fastened on one of her nipples, suckling her. She tilted her head back. His hands slid between their bodies, unfastening her pants and then slipping between her skin and her clothing. Delving deeply into the moist center of her body.

Jack set her on her feet and pushed her pants to the floor. They caught on her shoes until she kicked free of both the loafers and the pants. Jack unfastened his own pants and freed his erection. He lifted Anna again, and she wrapped her legs around his waist. He turned to rest his shoulders against the wall. She pulled his head to hers and thrust her tongue deep into his mouth as he entered her body.

She moved on him, setting a rhythm that took them both rapidly toward their climaxes. Jack's hands again roamed over her back, and she tightened and moved faster on him. He gripped her buttocks and held her still. Then he thrust up into her once, twice, and finally a third time, pushing her over the edge. She held tightly to him as she cried his name. He turned, and Anna was trapped between his driving body and the wall. He thrust into her one more time before his shout of completion echoed in the quiet apartment.

"Am I really yours?" she asked.

"Yes. You are. I love you, Anna Sterling. I know I'm not the guy you might have wanted to spend your life with, but—"

"Jack, you are exactly the kind of man I want to spend my life with. I love you, too."

He held her close and made love to her again. And Anna knew sometime in the middle of the night that she had found the man she'd always secretly been searching for. A man who would keep her safe but also let her have a life filled with excitement.

If you liked this story, pick up
INSTANT ATTRACTION,
by Jill Shalvis. . . .

"**W**hy are you in my bed?" he asked warily, as if maybe he'd put her there but couldn't quite remember.

He had a black duffel bag slung over a shoulder. Light brown hair stuck out from the edges of his knit ski cap to curl around his neck. Sharp green eyes were leveled on hers, steady and calm but irritated as he opened his denim jacket.

If he was an ax murderer, he was quite possibly the most attractive one she'd ever seen, which didn't do a thing for her frustration level. She'd been finally sleeping.

Sleeping!

He could have no idea what a welcome miracle that had been, dammit.

"Earth to Goldilocks." He waved a gloved hand until she dragged her gaze back up to his face. "Yeah, hi. My bed. Want to tell me why you're in it?"

"I've been sleeping here for a week." Granted, she'd had a hard time of it lately, but she definitely would have noticed *him* in bed with her.

"Who told you to sleep here?"

"My boss, Stone Wilder. Well, technically, Annie the chef, but—" She broke off when he reached toward her, clutching the comforter to her chin as if the down feathers could protect her, really wishing for that handy-dandy bat.

But instead of killing her, he hit the switch to the lamp on the nightstand and more fully illuminated the room as he dropped his duffel bag.

While Katie tried to slow her heart rate, he pulled off his jacket and gloves, and tossed them territorially to the chest at the foot of the bed.

His clothes seemed normal enough. Beneath the jacket he wore a fleece-lined sweatshirt opened over a long-sleeved brown Henley, half untucked over faded Levi's. The jeans were loose and low on his hips, baggy over unlaced Sorels, the entire ensemble revealing that he was in prime condition.

"My name is Katie Kramer," she told him, hoping he'd return the favor. "Wilder Adventures's new office temp." She paused, but he didn't even attempt to fill the awkward silence. "So that leaves you . . ."

"What happened to Riley?"

"Who?"

"The current office manager."

"I think she's on maternity leave."

"That must be news to his wife."

She met his cool gaze. "Okay, obviously I'm new. I don't know all the details since I've only been here a week."

"Here, being my cabin, of course."

"Stone told me that the person who used to live here had left."

"Ah." His eyes were the deepest, most solid green she'd ever seen as they regarded her. "I did leave. I also just came back."

She winced, clutching the covers a little tighter to her chest. "So this cabin . . . Does it belong to an ax murderer?"

That tugged a rusty-sounding laugh from him. "Haven't sunk that low. Yet." Pulling off his cap, he shoved his fingers through his hair. With those sleepy-lidded eyes, disheveled hair, and at least two days' growth on his jaw, he looked big and bad and edgy—and quite disturbingly sexy with it. "I need sleep." He dropped his long, tough self to the chair by the bed, as if so weary he could no longer stand. He set first one and then the other booted foot on the mattress, grimacing as if he were hurting, though she didn't see any reason for that on his body as he settled back, lightly linking his hands together low on his flat abs. Then he let out a long, shuddering sigh.

She stared at more than six feet of raw power and testosterone in disbelief. "You still haven't said who you are."

"Too Exhausted To Go Away."

She did some more staring at him. Staring and glaring, but he didn't appear to care. "Hello?" she said after a full moment of stunned silence. "You can't just—"

"Can. And am." And with that, he closed his eyes. "Night, Goldilocks."

And don't miss Diane Whiteside's latest,
KISSES LIKE A DEVIL,
available now from Brava. . . .

A single man stepped out of the station, isolated by a swirl of travelers. He was tall and broad-shouldered, clad entirely in black. His broad-brimmed hat readily identified him as an American, a rarity here in Eisengau despite its famous summer music festival and military maneuvers. His clothes were well made yet neither dandified nor a uniform. Straight black hair brushed his collar, and his skin was tanned golden brown from the sun, something seldom seen amid these stone walls. His blade-sharp nose, high cheekbones, and stubborn jaw could have been carved by a master sculptor.

He paused on the top of the steps to look around, graceful as a hawk scanning a meadow, yet utterly un-self-conscious. His brilliant blue eyes flashed over the crowd like light passing through the finest stained glass—and lingered briefly on the old pension, where Meredith stood.

Her breath caught in her throat. How many newspaper articles about American adventurers had she devoured? How many cheap novels about men like him had she bartered for? And to finally see one in the flesh . . .

Morro thrust his muzzle between the banisters and took a long, considering sniff.

Despite any claim to logic, Meredith opened her mouth to hail the American.

A British officer, shorter, stockier, and using a cane, rushed up to him. The healthier man slapped him warmly on the shoulder, his face lighting up in welcome—and broke the thread holding her attention.

She closed her eyes for a moment and jerked herself back to the relentless present.

Keep an eye out for
THE EDUCATION OF MADELINE,
Beth Williamson's Brava debut,
coming next month!

She made excuses to herself to visit him during the day when she was home. The hours at the bank gave her time to cool herself off, but then there were the times she was home and temptation was within reach. Each time, no matter if he wore his shirt or not, her heart and her body reacted as one. Reaching for him, wanting him. Needing to know what it felt like to touch him. What it felt like for him to touch her. Her experience was limited to simple kissing and hugging, but she could imagine quite a bit more. Especially with the help of the medical texts she'd read. Although none of them quite explained the exact details of fornication, she was fairly certain she had figured it out.

Now she couldn't wait to try it. If only she hadn't agreed to give Teague a week to decide. A week was too long. Far too long. She should have given him one day. No more. She had to find some way to distract herself from *thinking* about bedding him. An idea struck her.

Do you play any games, Teague?" Maddie asked as they left the dining room after supper.

He didn't answer, so she turned to look at him. A mischievous grin played around those beautiful lips, and one eyebrow arched over humor-filled eyes. "What kind of games?"

Madeline felt a bit flustered and she hoped it didn't reflect in her cheeks. She didn't want him to know that her self-control was melting like an icicle in July.

"Checkers, chess, backgammon. Those kinds of games."

When his grin turned into a full-blown smile, Madeline gripped the doorjamb to stay upright. She thought she was prepared. She was so very wrong. That smile was devastating. It lit up his whole face, made his eyes crinkle at the corners, and turned her into a puddle of unrequited passion.

"No, but I play a mean game of poker. Do you play?"

Madeline shook her head disappointed. That canceled her distraction idea.

"Would you like to learn?"

She felt an urge to blurt, "No!" but grabbed it before it could be let loose. The proper lady wasn't going to make the decisions this time. Proper ladies may not play poker, but Maddie Brewster was going to learn.

After searching for thirty minutes, they found a deck of cards in her father's old desk. Teague suggested they play in the kitchen since it was in the back of the house and relatively private.

When they settled at the table, the lamplight threw a cozy glow over the room. Madeline watched Teague's hands, fascinated by how quickly he shuffled the cards. His fingers were lithe and strong at the same time. She wondered how those fingers would feel on her skin, making her temperature rise degree by degree.

Teague explained a game called five-card stud. The rules were a bit complex, but Madeline understood most of them. He let her play a couple of practice hands, and then they started to play in earnest.

Madeline lost five hands in a row before she started to

really enjoy playing the game. She won the next hand. Teague actually looked surprised. "Very good, Maddie. You're getting the hang of it."

Madeline smiled. "I think I understand why gamblers like to play this so much. Can we gamble too?"

Teague threw back his head and laughed. It was the first time she'd heard him laugh, and the rough, raspy sound of it did something strange to her equilibrium. "Don't you think gambling is the root of all evil?"

"No, I don't. I've seen the root of evil, and it's definitely not poker."

He looked like he wanted to respond, but he didn't. He shrugged. "I don't have money to play for."

Madeline watched his hands as he shuffled the cards again.

"How about we play for truths?" he said without looking up.

"Truths?"

"Yes, each time one of us wins a hand, we get to ask the other a question, and the loser must tell the truth."

His hands shuffled faster. By the time the cards started flying off the deck, his fingers were a blur of motion. In a few seconds, five cards lay in front of her.

"I'll play for truths. There isn't much I've got to hide, anyway."

Madeline lost the first truth hand.

"Are you ready for the first question?" he asked with a small grin.

"Yes, I'm ready."

"Why did you paint your house blue?"

It was her turn to laugh. "I thought you were going to ask me what color my bloomers are."

His eyebrows rose. "Now you've spoiled it. That was my next question."

"I painted it blue because it is my favorite color, and I wasn't allowed to wear anything that bright. After my father died, I indulged myself."

He nodded. "That answers why it's so damn bright."

She laughed and waved her hands at the cards. "Deal again, Teague. I'm itching to ask you a truth question."

This time, Madeline won. She pondered her question for several minutes, earning a sigh and rolling eyes from the sore loser.

"Why didn't you say yes to my proposition to bed me?"

He clearly hadn't been expecting a personal question like that. The cards he'd been shuffling fell out of his hand like an explosion, raining down all over the table and floor. "I had to stop myself from saying yes too quickly."

Heat pooled low and insistent in her belly, and a throbbing began between her legs. "Does this mean you're saying yes to my . . . proposal?" she asked. Her mouth felt as dry as cotton. "I mean, it sounds as if you're going to say yes."

He stood abruptly, and she could see the outline of his penis clearly in his pants. My, oh my! That certainly was a large-looking organ. Much larger than the ones in the drawings in the book.

Teague let the rest of the cards fall from his hands and he came around the side of the table. The primal way he walked was enough to make her nipples pucker. He clearly wanted her. *Her*: Madeline Brewster!

When he reached her side, he knelt down on the floor next to her and cupped her face in his big hands. "Why me?"

She shrugged, somehow. "I need a big man. "I'm not . . . petite or feminine like most women. I didn't want my teacher to feel embarrassed by the size difference if I was bigger. You . . . you're bigger than me. And . . ."

"And?"

"Just looking at you makes my body hum."

His pupils widened, and he licked his lips.

He's going to kiss me!

Madeline closed her eyes. She expected his lips on hers. What she didn't expect was feather-light kisses along her brow, down her nose, across her cheekbones, to her chin. Small, jittery kisses that made her ache that much more. "Hurry up and kiss me," she demanded.

He chuckled against the corner of her mouth. "If you want me to be your teacher, you're going to have to be the student. Can you hand over the reins, Maddie girl?"

Madeline thought long and hard about that question. It wasn't a matter of being under his thumb like her father. It was trusting that he would teach her what she wanted to know without doubting or interfering in his methods. "Yes," she breathed.

She felt him smile. "Good. Now just close your eyes and feel. This is lesson number one."

"Wait! Does this mean yes?"